"Eve," I moan, "I can't do this much longer."

"Good," she says. "Say it."

"You feel so good," I breathe.

"Say it," she says, searching deep in my soul.

"Ohhh..."

"Say it." She's shaking my very bones.

"I love you I love you."

"I love you, Sunny," she whispers, and then I lose track of time, of where she ends and I begin, of what's her and what's me, for looking into her eyes all I can see is her looking back at me and me back at her and on and on and on, forever, infinity.

Dreamcatcher

Lori Byrd

Huntington, New York

Rising Tide Press
5 Kivy Street
Huntington Station, NY 11746
(516) 427-1289

Printed in the United States on acid-free paper

Publisher's note:
All characters, places and situations in this book are fictitious and any resemblance to persons (living or dead) is purely coincidental.

Publisher's Acknowledgments:
The publisher is grateful for all the support and expertise offered by the members of its editorial board: Bobbi Bauer, Adriane Balaban, Beth Heyn, Hat Edwards, Pat G, Marianne Miller and Marian Satriani. Special thanks to Joyce Honorof, M.D., for her excellent technical assistance. Thanks, also, to Edna G. for believing in us, and to the feminist and gay bookstores for being there.

First printing August, 1995
10 9 8 7 6 5 4 3 2 1

Edited by Hat Edwards
Book cover art: Denise St. John

Byrd, Lori 1952-
Dreamcatcher/Lori Byrd
p.cm

ISBN 1-883061-06-7 LC 94-074073

Acknowledgments

Thank you, editor-from-heaven Harriet Edwards, for your wisdom and excellence.

Thank you, Alice Frier and Lee Boojamra, for your clear vision and steadfast principles.

Thank you, Cindy Pursell, for your help with manuscript preparation.

And thanks to all the unseen hands, surely at work.

1

Kim is leaving, going back home to L.A. for a summer internship. We've shared an apartment in this rickety old house on Kentucky Street for three years now. I'm a poetry major, she's an art and design major. We'll be seniors in the fall, and after we graduate we'll probably go our separate ways.

Her faded green Honda is packed for the trip. We hug and say goodbye. My black and white border collie, Bennington, looks on with arched eyebrows, probably remembering the hot empty silence of high ceilings and hardwood floors and the sadness of certain hours from other summers past.

☾ ☾ ☾

Diane, my neighbor across the alley, is having a cookout. Her yard is filled with people. Some of them are professors or grad students that I recognize from school, but a lot of them are strangers, and most of them seem drunk or stoned, lolling around in cliques talking professions—clinical psychologists here, lawyers there, editors, real estate agents, and so on.

I am here because I've just finished painting Diane's house and she insists I join the party. I end up staying until late, and many of the guests have gone. A few of us are playing poker in the kitchen. I get up for more beers and someone slinks up behind me and says breathily:

"I'll bet you just love to mow lawns, don't you?"

Hers is the kind of voice that might be associated with 1-900 numbers: it is like silk on my breasts and fur on my fingertips. I whirl around and find myself face-to-face with Eve Phillips, editor, literary agent, ex-lover of Diane.

Eve runs her business out of her home and she's been unable to find anyone reliable enough to care for her yard. Says it looks so trashy having weeds and vines all grown up around the front porch. She'll provide the lawn mower—all I have to do is show up in the morning. Is it a deal?

☾☾☾

It's a white, two-story stone and stucco hacienda in an older neighborhood near campus. Oaks and sycamores form a canopy over the street so that as you walk along the sidewalk, it's like being in the midst of a thick green tunnel filled with echoing songbirds and shrieking, jabbering children busy at play.

I am knocking on Eve's screen door at ten in the morning as clouds of incense billow from her window. Her giant black and white cat, Olga, snoozes on the porch swing. Music is blaring. It sounds like "Sweet Taboo." Eve glides to the door wearing a blue kimono and sunglasses. She's lighting a cigarette.

"Hi, kiddo, come on in. Want some coffee?"

"No thanks."

"Scotch?"

"No."

The phone rings. Eve motions for me to have a seat, excuses herself, answers the phone.

"Eve Phillips," she says. She sips something brown from a crystal glass. It looks like oil. It might be Kahlua.

"You must be joking," she says. "I applied for that position two years ago."

A pause.

"I see. Oh, really. Well, that's very kind of you. An

interview? Thursday?" She catches my eye, winks.

"No, I'm sorry, that's just too soon. A week from Friday? I'm afraid that's out of the question. Convenient? Oh, how about two years from now? Then maybe that'll give you time to update your files!" And with that, she hangs up.

"How come they never hire you when you're desperate, alone, and suicidal?" she asks, looking over at me. "No, they want you to suffer, they file you away and let your application ripen for a year or two. It's a control thing. Shit, I'm so glad to be out of that rat-race."

She chuckles. "Hey, Sunny, I'll bet you're here to mow the lawn, aren't you?"

☾ ☾ ☾

While Eve fixes us a snack of shrimp scampi and salad, she tells me she started her own business because she was sick and tired of working for assholes. She makes most of her profit from putting together resumés and newsletters, she explains, though she's also an agent, editor, arbitrageur, procurer—I'm not sure what else. What I am sure of is that since I mowed her lawn two weeks ago she has appointed herself my manager. It's a fairly simple arrangement—I show up at her house every morning and she provides me with a list of lawns to mow. The list keeps growing every day, and that first cup of coffee with Eve always gets my day off to an uproarious start.

☾ ☾ ☾

I've come home to my bare, roasting apartment, worn out from mowing lawns all day, but unable to sleep. The radio next door is blaring. If my roommate Kim were here, we'd be up talking. We'd be on the steps of the back porch catching the cool breeze and

I'd tell her about Eve. I'd tell her about going to work this morning. I'd tell her about this image I can't get out of my mind.

It's an image of Eve, and she's in the kitchen, on the phone, bent down peering into the refrigerator, wearing that blue kimono she wears, and she looks up as I walk in. She winks. Her hair is tied loosely with a piece of yarn and strands of it fall down her neck and across her shoulders. Her eyes, so large and hollow, pierce me with their intensity. I remember that morning's telephone conversation.

"Find somebody else, then. That's my price."

The refrigerator door whams shut. She points to a basket of fruit on the table, motions for me to eat.

"Fuck Kramer. You want half-assed proposals? Then fine."

She sweeps across the floor on long legs like—not a racehorse, more like a deer, I think. She stands at the counter pouring coffee, backlit, pale and slender..

"Hell, no, that's ridiculous, who told you that? Sheila? Really?" She plunks a full coffee mug down in front of me. Pulls a pen from her pocket, scribbles some figures on her palm, negotiating wildly.

"Yah, okay. Tell him Tuesday. Sure. Bye."

As soon as she hangs up, the phone rings again.

"Eve Phillips," she says, disappearing down the hallway. I hear the sound of bath water running.

I can't help imagining her in there: silk robe hanging on the back of the door, lacy panties in a corner, a breeze ruffling the curtain as she slips into that warm, fragrant, bubbling water, graceful as a dragonfly, her shoulders pale and delicate, slightly freckled, beads of sweat down the small of her back.

I think I have a pretty good idea what Kim might say about all this, but Kim is gone, and so I toss and turn all night, chasing shadows in my sleep.

☾ ☾ ☾

It's her nose, I think, above the roar of the mower, working on my fifth or sixth lawn of the day. More than anything else, it's her nose I admire. How would I describe it to someone who's never seen it, or to someone not the connoisseur that I am? To one not discriminating or appreciative of the subtleties amongst olfactory organs (snouts, beaks, bills, nasal cavities), a nose by any other name would surely smell as sweet.

I think I've inhaled too much gasoline. Or maybe it's the heat—so hot today even the dogs are lying in comas. Kids have abandoned their wading pools, fleeing indoors, and birds huff and puff, their beaks wide open. Maybe I should have worn my hat.

I try to find the precise words.

Patrician? Aristocratic?

"A fine, straight nose."

Regal? Sublime? Imperial? Distinctive? Impeccable? Flawless? Perfect? It's a perfect nose, for certain. But how to convey that using poetics and literary gusto? How to relate with eloquence its majesty as seen in profile?

"A singularly graceful nose."

Not very original. It's a strong nose, sure. Noble, stately. Yes, but what does it *look* like? Well, it must be examined within the context of her face. Which is...? Refined. Artful. Well-wrought. (I give up.)

☾ ☾ ☾

I'm so tired I probably won't even dream tonight. I've come by to drop off Eve's lawn mower and we sit on the porch for a while, talking and listening to the crickets.

At least by not dreaming there's less chance of my having that nightmare. The one where I drown. I've had it since childhood, but most especially lately.

"The thing is..." I rattle on, thinking out loud, "the thing is, I love dreaming. Even though Aunt Buck says the only thing that ever comes to a dreamer is dreams, I get some of my best ideas in my sleep. Sometimes I lie in bed at night and tell myself what to dream. Occasionally I'm able to realize when I'm dreaming, and thereby control it."

Eve nods, finishes her cigarette and the last of her drink. She's wearing a thin tank top that doesn't begin to cover her breasts when she stretches. It's time for me to go.

"Once I dreamed," she says with great effort, slurring, running her fingers along my arm, "Once I dreamed that Jupiter fell out of orbit and came reeling so close to Earth we could look up and see the striped awnings on all the tiny little buildings. And all around us the sky shimmered like neon."

☾ ☾ ☾

The water is bubbling and blue and so shot through with light I can't tell which way is up. I swim one way and then another, but can't seem to find the surface. My ears pound, my lungs are ready to burst.

Recklessly, I inhale, then regret what I've done. But wait—it's not so bad. Water tastes like air. I inhale again, swim some more, and now I know I'm dreaming.

So I decide—and why not?—to become a dolphin. My arms and legs withdraw into a tight, slick, gray-white body dancing streamlined above the waves. Rattles, pops, and squeaks escape me. Such energy! What sensation! I can scarcely contain my exuberance.

My skin's a total receptor, more like brain than flesh; it feels the smack of the Atlantic, sees each drop of water in this interior sea lighted by churning seagulls. It tallies taste and smell, hearing gulls squawk like musical aardvarks miles and miles across the water.

Above me, but beyond the range of perception, the sun is a color stretching more and more as dripping, scattered, slow-glowing honey. I dive, my skin hearing the rocks, the tides, the sunken ships, smelling the dark, the light, the shimmer of summer storms.

Speeding deeper, darker, tiny fish like shadows steaming by, I dip, turn, and with a flick of my tongue swallow a snack that tastes like—like sushi!

☾ ☾ ☾

The next morning I'm sitting beside Eve on her porch swing as she goes over a list of lawns I am to mow today. Business has really mushroomed. We watch a family of bluejays dive-bomb Olga. Unconcerned, she sprawls in the grass, drooling and slurping over a new catnip toy.

Eve asks if I had any interesting dreams last night. Would she really be interested in my dolphin story, I wonder, or is she just making conversation? So I'm just getting ready to tell her about it when the phone rings. I shrug. Eve goes inside to answer it. The cordless phone is broken. I think she got drunk last night and backed over it with her car.

I take my list, fold it up, put it in the pocket of my shorts, and head down the street with the lawn mower. My first stop is Patty Euphoria's, a big old red-and-gray house with a ratty yard and a broken-down fence with slats missing. Patty runs Patty's Fried Chicken downtown, across from the courthouse. I've heard she can bench press four hundred and fifty-five pounds. She also runs a thriving bootleg wine and beer operation out of her basement.

☾ ☾ ☾

Bennington lifts an ear, looks over at me, and barks.

"Knock knock," calls Diane from the back porch.

"Hi. Come on in," I holler. I hear the screen door squeak open and shut as she bangs in. I'm in the living room stretched out in Kim's blue recliner, the most comfortable seat in my apartment. The fan is on.

Diane breezes in, hands me a can of Coke with frost

running down the sides. Gratefully I take it. Beads of water drip onto the spiral notebook in my lap and I quickly close it.

"What cha working on?" asks Diane.

"Just scribbling," I say. Actually I've been sitting here writing verses about Eve for the past hour-and-a-half. "You look nice. What's up?"

Since Diane quit her reporting job at the paper in order to write fiction full time, she usually runs around in jeans or shorts and t-shirts. Today she's in skirt and heels and a white linen jacket.

"I come to ask your hand in marriage, O Fairest," she says.

"Ha! Let me guess. The Jeep won't start."

She looks a little embarrassed. "No, I've locked myself out of the house. I was wondering if you'd come over and shimmy through my window."

I liked the part about marriage a lot better, I tell her. "Sure," I grin. "Let's go."

Bennington zips across the alley with us and I scoot through the narrow pantry window, slip down the hall, and unlock the door. Diane says she's having me a key made tomorrow.

She flings her sunglasses and earrings on the kitchen table and halfway to the bedroom she's kicked off her shoes and is out of her skirt.

"Geez, what a day. Business lunch, meetings, contract approval, negotiations, what a bunch of crap. Sunny, will you fix me a drink?"

She thunders through the house and reappears in the kitchen minutes later, barefoot, in loose white shorts and a Bullwinkle t-shirt. She's flipping through her mail. I measure out the vodka, add ice.

"I saw Eve today down at Ryan's," she says. "Told me I should come by and see how you've transformed her yard. I hear you're in big demand as a gardener."

"What was she doing at Ryan's?"

"Well, as she puts it, 'getting properly gassed' for her

appointment with the IRS. I guess she's being audited."

"Yes, I heard. I hope it went well."

"Oh, it did. I saw her downtown afterwards. All taken care of. No problem. Can you believe it?"

"Wow," I say.

"You know, sometimes I really envy her."

"Funny. She says that about you too."

"Really?"

I nod, inscrutable.

"Sometimes I wonder what it'd be like to be so goddam detached all the time. Just give the old girl a little love, a lotta booze, and something to read...she's happy!"

I don't feel this is a very fair assessment of Eve, but I keep my mouth shut. After all, Diane's the one who lived with her for five years, not me. And I'm not exactly in a position to be objective.

☾ ☾ ☾

Tuesday morning rush hour looks rainy. Cars and trucks rumble past as I climb the steps to Eve's. I pick up the newspaper and open the screen door. Eve is having coffee at the table. I can't be sure, but I think she's smiling. Very unusual at this hour.

"You shit," she says.

"Now what?"

"You've been holding out on me."

"What're you talking about?" I'm confused.

"You just want to mow lawns for the rest of your life?"

"Nothing wrong with that," I say.

"Where's your ambition? You could've been helping *me* for the past month!"

"You're too bossy. I couldn't work with you."

"I am not, and of course you will. Starting tomorrow."

"Eve, I hate computers and desk work."

"No you don't. You'll do fine."

"Besides, I can't do what you do."

"And what do you think I do, kiddo? How do you think I got started in this business? I've been bluffing along nicely for two years now. I'm serious, Sunny. I really need the help."

"I'll think about it," I mutter on my way out the door. But I know I'll say OK.

This whole turn of events has come about just a little too smoothly, I'm thinking to myself. A couple of nights ago, in a generous mood, Eve volunteered to compose a resumé for me. I said I thought such things were redundant, superfluous, and usually fraudulent. After considering this for a moment, she agreed.

"But that's the fun of it!" she said, adding that it might be a good idea for me to get my vast and distinguished work history in order for when cold weather rolls around.

I had to admit she was probably right. So I went to the library and got a book and figured out how to write a resumé. No big deal. Then I worked up a rough draft and left it for her to spruce up on her word processor. And now it looks as if my mellow, laid-back days as a gardener are over.

Two lawns finished, and I feel like a bag of wet cement. As I begin my third lawn of the morning, my overactive imagination kicks in:

It's raining. I load Eve's mower into the trailer hooked behind my bike and skid two miles back to her place. By now it's pouring and the streets are starting to flood. I leave my bike and the mower in the garage and dart through the back door to the kitchen.

I am drenched. Eve asks if I'd like to take a shower. When I'm clean and dry, I put on a blue cotton blouse of hers and a pair of white shorts and we have lunch.

The house is very dark. Rain booms on the roof of the back porch like miniature kettle drums. A cool breeze blows through the windows and door, and the curtains are stirring like ghosts. We finish our meal in silence. Eve says the rain is making her sleepy. She takes my hand, and we go into the bedroom to lie down....

2

It's my first day with the Eve Phillips Agency and throngs of people fan in and out of the house. Just answering the phone is a full-time job. I am sequestered in a back room with just the word processor and copier so as to minimize the trauma. I hear Eve on the phone in the other room, recruiting some young butch named Whistles to take over my lawn-mowing route.

☾ ☾ ☾

Eve has been chatting with a client in the front office, and when I pass by the doorway I think it's Marilyn Hacker. Then I realize it's not, but it sure looks like her. Enough to take my breath away.

After the woman leaves, I tell Eve who I thought she was. She looks at me blankly.

"So? Who's Marilyn Hacker?"

"A poet," I say.

"Do you know her?"

"Well, no. But I know her work. She's incredible. She wrote this one piece, *Canzone,* about the many functions of the tongue...."

"Does she need an agent?" Eve wants to know.

"I doubt it. She's fairly well-published."

"Just checking. Hey, I didn't know you liked poetry."

"Well, sure. It's my major."

"How come?"

How come? I look at her blankly.

The phone rings. Another client bangs in. Olga lounges in a windowsill, blinking at the sun.

☾ ☾ ☾

It's Saturday morning. Eve hands me the car keys and asks if I'll go to the store and get her a good breakfast wine.

I like driving her car. It's an older black Mercedes 250, with squashed McDonald's cups everywhere, and books and magazines and old airline reservations all over the dash.

Later, when it's raining, we sit in the study with the windows open reading poetry out loud. Eve just loves *At The New World Donut Shop,* something by Patricia Traxler. She roars when I get to the part about the old man far back in a corner where things are really jumping.

"'Tell you what, tell you what, tell you what!'"

She cracks up and makes me read it over and over again.

☾ ☾ ☾

I'm trying to explain why I love poetry so much, but I'm not sure I'm doing a very good job. I use the word communion, for starters. I say it's a feeling of total communion, sometimes, with another's innermost being. I say it can be a form of intimacy; in fact, it's the most powerful form of intimacy I've ever experienced.

I say it's like love at first sight and I say it's like drugs, only better. I say it's a coded language, a shorthand to the mind and heart. I say how reading the work of a poet I love, first thing in the day, can be the most exciting thing I've ever known.

And I wait for Eve to tell me how weird or boring I am, or that I'm beyond dysfunctional. But she never does.

☾☾☾

There are two doors at the front of her house. One goes into the living room and the other, to the right, is the office entrance. In the office, Eve has her desk, computer, printer, copier, phone, and a bookcase. There are several hanging philodendron and airplane plants, a love seat and a wing-backed chair, and a couple of framed watercolors on the wall. Instead of carpeting there's a large brown-and-tan Oriental rug in the middle of the floor.

A sliding glass door, usually left open, separates the office and living room. There's a large stone fireplace in the living room, and an antique grandfather clock that Eve's father had shipped over from Switzerland. I've never met her father. Diane says he's a cardiologist in San Francisco.

Leading from the living room is the dining room, and next to that is the kitchen. Eve says the thing she regretted most about moving out of Diane's when they broke up was leaving behind that nice big kitchen. Though this one is by no means tiny, neither is it suited for an Olympic-caliber chef like Eve. When she gets totally burned out on word processing, and that might be any day now, she warns, she's starting her own restaurant. She's going to call it the Forbidden Fruit Café.

Off the kitchen is a hallway which leads to the bath and study. There's another, older computer in the study, as well as a TV, VCR, and an extremely comfortable old brown sofa.

Situated between the bathroom and the office is Eve's bedroom, which is an absolute wreck. I like to walk through here on my way to the bathroom just to inhale the smell of her Armani, and to check out her late-night reading material. She's big on *The Smithsonian* and *The Architectural Digest.*

Blue is Eve's favorite color and her sheets are solid, no flowers or prints. The antique brass bed is seldom made. On the nightstand next to it I see a copy of Amy Tan's *Joy Luck Club.* The bookmark changes place from time to time, so I know she's reading it.

Beside the doorway leading into the bathroom is a heavy old dresser of oak. In the middle of it sits a pile of clean laundry: jumbled towels and panties lie next to perfume bottles and old ash-trays and several empty bar glasses on coasters. In the bottom of one glass sits a crusty lemon wedge, and in another, what might be a calcified lime.

Off to one side, away from the clutter of her everyday life, are photographs of Eve's mother, her father, and her brother. There is a strong family resemblance. In one picture, Eve is leaning against her mother, their arms around each other as they stand beside the pool. Neither one looks at the camera. Eve gazes out across the water and a breeze is ruffling her dark, shoulder-length hair. She might be fourteen. Both are smiling. Mother faces daughter with an expression of pride and tenderness, like a lioness admiring her young cub.

In another, it is Christmas and the family is gathered in front of the tree. Eve sits in her father's lap, sharing his wide teddy-bear smile. She is wearing a red-and-white jumper, white lacy socks, and shiny black patent leather shoes. Her hair hangs loose around her shoulders with short, uneven bangs. A front tooth is missing.

Father is dressed in slacks and golf shirt. His eyes, so dark they appear black, shine like buttons. Eve's hand rests absently on his cheek, as if moments before they had been sharing a kiss.

Eve's mother holds Gerry in her lap, a chipmunk-cheeked toddler who stares dumbly, happily at his older sister. In his hand is a crumbling gingerbread man.

Mother smiles, and her teeth are very white. You can see that she is happy to be here with her husband and her children, all of them with dark, shiny hair, those arresting Phillips eyes, the well-bred grace of narrow bones. Yes, they are the perfect family.

Every day at 4:30, no matter what, Eve tunes in "Jeopardy." If she's in the middle of a rush job and can't go to the living room she'll turn the volume way up and sit with her back to the TV, yelling out answers:

"Who was Ophelia!"

"What is Old North Church!"

"Who are the Jetsons!"

The phone rings. I answer it. Eve is bellowing in the background.

"What is a snapping turtle!"

I put my hand over the mouthpiece. "Eve, it's Monroe calling about her thesis."

"*A Hundred and One Dalmatians*! Tell her it's ready. What is Egypt!"

The phone rings again. I take the call, one eye on the TV.

"—the legislative branch! Who was Hemingway!"

I join Eve in a showdown of out-shouting and outwitting each other during the Double Jeopardy round.

"Who is Nelson Mandela!"

"—iambic pentameter!"

"Who were the Weird Sisters!"

I'm pulling ahead, and Eve claps her hand over my mouth.

"Mmph mthp Bea Arthur!"

She wrestles me out of my seat, gets me down on the floor. The stakes are high because the loser has to drive downtown, make a bank deposit, then swing by the post office.

"—a minuet!"

I miss two categories because she has me in a half-nelson, with a pillow over my face.

"Toll House cookies!"

Someone's on the porch, getting ready to come into the office. I scramble out from beneath Eve; she swoops to her feet, both of us red-faced, out of breath.

Eve politely but hastily finishes with her client in time

for the final category, which is science.

"This Polish scientist, known as the founder of modern astronomy, died in 1543," says Alex Trebek.

"Galileo!" shrieks Eve.

"Rrrrrnnt!" I buzz. "Your answer is totally, totally incorrect, Ms. Phillips. Ha ha."

"Is not."

"Is too. You're off by about a hundred years."

"Oh, yeah? Then who is it?"

"Copernicus. Galileo was Italian."

"And of course," crows Alex Trebek, "the correct answer is Copernicus."

Heh heh.

"I'll thank you not to sneer," Eve replies. She quickly suggests we go to the bank and post office together, then she'll take me out for dinner. She eyes my ratty t-shirt and bare feet.

"We gotta get you some new threads, kiddo. Doesn't your boss ever pay you?"

"Some of us just don't have your flair for accessories," I shrug.

Eve's wearing a blue denim work shirt with the sleeves ripped out, raggedy jeans, and thongs...

It's Friday. It has been a grueling week.

3

"Where do these ideas of yours come from?" Eve is asking, wearing a mask of shock and dismay.

I don't know whether to run or laugh or cry. She has just finished reading a handful of poems I wrote last summer, along with a few others that have been lying around my room since Christmas. They remind me of tangled spaghetti, or worse sometimes, deflated Jell-O.

I tell Eve I don't know where my ideas come from. Does anyone? They're like helium-filled balloons or butterflies that defy apprehension. A poem is like the wind. It comes from a far-off place and we feel it.

"Hmmm," she nods. "Are there any more of these?"

"Boxes full."

"I think I'd like to see them."

☾ ☾ ☾

This morning, while Eve and I are working, I mention a dream that I had during the night about Pie Lady. Pie Lady's a descendant of Mayflower people, I explain. For years her family mistakenly believe her to be crazy because she seldom speaks, and when she does, it's apt to be to trees, or stones, or chipmunks. She leads a very cloistered life.

But one day she's puttering around in the kitchen and she bakes a pie. Everyone is astounded because it is the most magnificent pie ever created. She bakes another. And another. Soon her angelfood pies are legendary.

Year after year the summer people make pilgrimages to her door. Pie Lady's pies are imbued with the power to touch people's hearts, change their lives. So exquisite are her pies, so full of magic and love, that they tend to float out of windows by themselves. It is also said that white doves can be seen floating up from the pies, disappearing far away into the clouds.

Eve's reaction to this serendipitous tale surprises me. She tells me to set aside the Aztec Bodybuilding Club newsletter I am designing and go write down everything I've told her.

Well, all right. So I come out here in her back yard, beneath my favorite maple, and I watch the leaves sift down one by one like notes in music, shimmering beneath what look like wings of angels disappearing far, far off in the sky. And I begin to write.

☾ ☾ ☾

I stop in at Diane's and find her reading her fan mail. She lets it accumulate at the post office and goes through it when she has time. Sacks full of it rest on the floor at her feet.

She has just completed her fourth novel, a sort of disjointed philosophical Lesbian action fantasy called *Higher Octaves.*

"This is great," she says, reading a large, spidery script on perfumed lavender stationery. "Bless her heart. This darling woman wants to know if I'm a Sagittarius and would I be interested in meeting her for cocktails at George's in Fayetteville some time? *I love* shit like this."

Who wouldn't?

"And hey," she continues, "she says she's five-three, has big brown eyes, curly red hair, writes poetry...now wait a minute. Sunny, did you write this?"

No, but I wish I had. A few gag letters would keep her on her toes.

"She's probably not as adorable as I am," I say.

"Too bad she didn't enclose a snapshot." Diane replaces the letter in the envelope and reaches for another. "Oh by the way, speaking of adorable, I know someone who thinks you're kinda cute."

I'm browsing through the new issue of *People.* After what I hope is an appropriate pause, I ask "Who?"

No reply. "Oh, my God," she squeals.

I cut her a sidelong glance, see that she's reading another letter.

"Oh, Lordy." She fans herself dramatically. "Get the gurney, hon. I'm gonna swoon." She stuffs the page back in the envelope, says "That one's for later!" and asks if I'd mind fixing her a drink.

I get up and come to the kitchen, rattle around measuring out Finlandia.

"Oh, my," she says, reading. "Oh, my my..."

"Yeeeeees?"

"...thinks I'm a visionary...admires my intellectual prowess...my unabashed autoeroticism!"

"Cool," I shout from the kitchen. "So who is it thinks I'm kinda cute, Diane?"

"—brutally elegant...a lithe goddess in the endless wet thick cosmos—"

I return to the living room and place a huge tumbler of vodka beside her.

"Thanks, hon. Sunny?"

"Hmmm?"

"Be honest. Do I weave a quiet and mysterious spell of enchantment?"

"Oh, yes," I sigh. "And your freshness of perception is pure ecstasy."

She reaches around and clobbers me with her foot.

"Who is it, Diane?"

"Oh, it's Eve," she says casually. "Eve thinks you're pretty special."

"Really?"

She winks, takes a long, thoughtful sip, goes back to her mail.

☾ ☾ ☾

Tonight I'm sitting in the Blue Onion, a little lounge off-campus where the sandwiches are good and the music isn't too loud. Sort of a neighborhood bar. I don't come here much during the school year because it gets mobbed by sorority and fraternity kids. But in the summer it takes on a different character. Even the owners leave in the summer, to go wherever they go, and during that time it's managed by a colorful local figure, a townie known as Snappy Pat.

Snappy Pat is a box. That's a tactful way of saying she's burly, and to say she's burly is an understatement. For example, once when her truck had a blowout, she didn't need a jack to change it.

Things are slow tonight, which is fine with me. I just want to eat my sandwich and drink some beer and then go home. I don't care much for shooting pool or playing pinball or wasting time on video games. I'm just not much of a bar person. I'd rather be out in the fresh air.

Snappy Pat eases over, asks how I'm doing, how school's going, etc. She tells me she's buying some property on Fox Hollow Road out north of town in that forested area where a lot of the really politically and culturally correct types are gathering. She's very excited.

"Cool," I say. I get the impression her new lover is financing everything. She tells me about their recent backpacking adventure and how it seemed to rain constantly at the higher altitudes, and then coming back home, how the truck hydroplaned and swerved onto the median, and then jackknifed and hit another car. So her truck's in the shop now and the insurance company's saying those new radials she bought for the trip were defective. Yeah, Pat, I'm thinking, you were probably just too stoned to be driving.

Snappy Pat tells me they'll be having a big housewarming celebration after the cabin deal goes through, and I'm invited, and she's heard I'm doing some work for Eve Phillips lately.

Yes, I say.

Am I liking it?

"Yeah. Long hours, but Eve's a pretty good boss. She's a lot of fun."

How is Diane handling it?

What do you mean?

You *did* know they were lovers?

"Well, sure. But that was four or five years ago."

"And Eve hasn't been with anyone else since the breakup," says Pat. "I hear they watch each other like hawks. You know, Diane has a wild streak."

"Diane? Nah."

Pat eyes me with amusement. "So she never told you about what happened up in Michigan?"

Evidently I look blank, or stupid, or something.

"Me and my big mouth. Forget it," she says.

"Come on, Pat."

"You honestly never heard about what happened when she was teaching?"

"No."

"If I tell you, do you promise to forget where you heard it?"

"I promise."

So, after a little more coaxing, Pat tells me how Diane developed quite a fondness for several of her journalism students and eventually got caught and was fired. That pretty much wrecked her academic career. She finally landed a job here, as a reporter for the paper. She met Eve, who was a law student at the time.

This surprises me. I didn't know Eve went to law school.

"Only for about an hour," laughs Pat. "No, it was a little longer than that. Maybe a year. She dropped out, worked as a travel agent, lived with Diane. Then Diane got to fooling around again."

"I just can't believe it," I say.

"Believe it," she says flatly. "But yeah, Diane has changed a lot since then. I think losing Eve really knocked some sense into her."

☾ ☾ ☾

It bothers me to think that I've known Diane for this long and have been unaware of something so major. When I get home and see her light burning across the alley, I decide to pay her a middle-of-the-night visit, thought I'm not sure exactly why.

I see her through the kitchen window as I come around the side of the house, TV on, computer keyboard in her lap, glass of wine on the table. I knock and she gets up to let me in.

"Sunny honey," she greets me, sounding fairly smashed, running her hands up my arms, stopping at the shoulders. "Nice muscles."

She tells me she's glad I've stopped by, asks if I'd like some wine.

"No," I say, rummaging through her refrigerator for a beer.

We go into the living room where the aquarium bubbles brightly. Diane stretches out on the floor, complaining of a stiff neck, asks if I'd mind giving her a massage.

"There's lotion in the bedroom," she says, "on the night-stand."

I ask, can't I finish my beer first?

"No."

I make a crack about feeble-minded old Pulitzer Prize winners and set my cold beer right in the middle of her back. She jumps up, reaches around playfully, grabs me by the seat of my pants.

"In the bedroom. On the nightstand," she insists. "Now."

Okay, okay. I get up, go into the bedroom for the

lotion. On my way back Diane suggests I put on some music.

"*Tina Turner's Greatest Hits* would be fine."

"Will there be anything else, Your Majesty?" I ask.

"Yes. Would you please bring me a sheet to lie on?"

When we're finally settled, Diane pulls off her blouse and I go to work on her neck, back and shoulders.

I'm surprised at how soft she is. She has broad shoulders and lean, muscular biceps, with a very fine layer of blonde hair all over. It reminds me of the tiny hairs on bees' legs that they use to gather pollen. I run my hands over her thighs and forearms and watch the static electricity make her bee hair stand up.

I feel her starting to relax. A wind chime *chings* somewhere in the house, probably brushed by Apostrophe or Catastrophe, her Siamese cats. She tells me the reason she's so tense has to do with working such long hours on last-minute revisions before *Higher Octaves* can go to press. The manuscript is just about ready; she, her editor and her publisher have finally agreed on specifics, and the book should be out in six to nine months. The jacket design is over on the table, she says. I slip over and look.

It shows Earth as seen from a distance, surrounded by glowing auras of lime green, hot pink and orange sherbet, gradually shading into cinnamon. "*Higher Octaves,*" it says, "*is a delightful Lesbian romp set in a futuristic paradise.*" Diane mentions the cover painting was done by Mary Elgin, a local artist, someone she thinks I should meet.

"Far out," I smile, turning it over and over in my hands, wondering just what it would feel like to be a successfully published author. A little envious, I finish my beer, and notice it's late.

"Hey, Sunny, that was heaven," Diane tells me, flexing her back, stretching. "I feel about a hundred and fifty years younger, kiddo. Thanks."

I realize that she and Eve are the only people who ever call me kiddo.

"Another beer?" she asks.

"No thanks, I'd better go."

"Want to stay here with me tonight?"

She's only asking because she knows I don't have air conditioning.

"Better not," I say.

"Why?"

"I need to get home and feed Bennington. I've been neglecting her lately. And I need a bath."

"Fine. Scoot over there and feed your dog, bring her back with you, and take your bath here."

When I think of the alternative—roasting in my apartment, with Bennington sprawled on the floor panting, and my new upstairs neighbors pounding away at sex all night—I know it would be insane to refuse.

☾ ☾ ☾

The morning glories we planted along the front of Eve's house are finally blooming. Some are blue, some are violet or delicate pink, and some are magenta fiestas with stripes of white chiffon. All are dazzling. I greet them on my way up the steps and they seem to hear me and nod, swaying in the breeze.

Eve, however, does not greet me. I feel a definite chill in the air as I walk in the door. She's sitting at the word processor, dressed in faded Levis and a pink, orange and lavender tie-dyed tank top—no robe or sunglasses this morning.

My coffee mug is not sitting in its usual place on the table. There's no music playing. Even Olga's lying low.

"Hi," I venture. "Beautiful day, isn't it?"

"Never mind the trick questions, Sunny. I need you to run some errands. The list is on the table."

She fishes the car keys from her purse, tosses me a couple of twenties.

"And fill the car up while you're out. And have it washed.

And waxed." She goes back to work.

Woo. I scan the long, convoluted list she's made and already my head begins to ache.

"And call me before you come back," she adds, "There might be more by then."

Gosh, Eve, maybe you should do some acid to mellow out, I think.

I go back outside and around to the breezeway where Olga is nestled on the hood of the car. She wakes and scrambles off, tail fluffed, when I get in and start it up. As I back the Mercedes out the drive I realize I don't look forward to running all over town on two hours of sleep.

At lunch time, when I get back to Eve's, I notice Diane's Jeep parked in the drive, so I park on the street. On my way to the porch I remember Eve telling me to call before coming back, which I've forgotten to do. The hell with it, I decide. I've got a headache.

Halfway up the steps I hear fighting inside.

"I can't believe it! Now you're fucking Sunny!"

"Eve, now stop it. You know better than that. Calm down—"

The front door flies open. Olga scampers out, followed by Diane. Diane ducks to avoid a flying object—a loaded ashtray—which clonks me in the face at the same time she skids into the porch railing and knocks me down. I careen sideways down the steps with Olga hissing and spitting when I land on top of her.

"Good God, Eve, you've hurt her!" yells Diane, rushing over to me.

I can't see anything out of my right eye. My head is pounding. Blood is everywhere. From my left eye I see children in swimsuits huddling around, watching us curiously from the sidewalk. Diane snatches a towel from one of them and places it over my eye.

"Yep. Think you better get her to the hospital," advises

Fran, who has suddenly appeared out of nowhere. A retired nurse, Fran is Eve's frisky seventy-something neighbor. Her miniature poodle J.J. barks frenziedly.

A snazzily attired businessman is mincing across the lawn.

"Excuse me," he says, "I'm looking for the Eve Phillips Agency?"

"Help me get her in the car," Diane barks at him.

Bleeding and protesting, I'm loaded into the back of the Jeep. By now a small crowd has gathered.

"By the way, Eve, I'm not fucking her," snaps Diane, as the engine roars to life.

The businessman's eyebrows twitch.

"Oh, my," clucks Fran, standing aside as Eve comes running over to the car.

Eve yanks open the passenger door and jumps inside as Diane screeches down the drive.

The last thing I remember is the two of them arguing, red-faced, as we bullet dizzily down a tree-lined street. I realize that this fight really has little, if anything, to do with me.

4

Eve says there's nothing like blackberry wine for curing an upset stomach. She's sitting on the porch with a jug of Patty Euphoria's home brew when I arrive at work. She's wearing her blue kimono, and judging from her eyes, she hasn't slept.

The morning glory vines have grown up so thick around the sides of the porch that it resembles a green cave, blocking any view from the street. It's probably a good thing. Clients might get apprehensive at the agency being run by a pajama-clad wino.

"Hi, kiddo." She greets me with one of her dazzling smiles.

I'm thinking how I'd just love to have my way with her, drunk, right here on the porch.

"Coffee should be ready," she says. "Or would you prefer a snap of this?" She holds out the container to me. It's strong. I can smell it.

"Sure, I'll try a snap," I grin, and join Eve on the swing. She puts an arm around me, kisses me on the cheek.

"I love you, baby," she says.

"I love you, too," I say cheerily, taking a swig from the bottle. My head fogs from the sweet burning fire.

"Good, isn't it?" she smiles.

The phone rings. Eve reaches down and picks it up off the floor.

"Eve Phillips," she says, listens a while, then abruptly hangs up.

"Who was that?"

"Don't know," she laughs. "I hung up before they could say."

It rings again. Eve picks up the phone and fires it over the porch railing into a hedge.

"I'm sick of being responsible," she says. "Let them write their own damn resumés."

Far out, I'm thinking, and have another sip of wine.

Eve stands, takes me by the hand.

We go inside. To the bedroom. We are standing next to the unmade bed. She opens her kimono, takes my hands in hers, places them on her warm, soft belly. We kiss. We...

Bennington is barking and prodding me with her nose. I wake up disoriented from crazy dreams and I hear someone hammering at the front door. The digital clock next to my bed says Saturday, 8:35 a.m.

I get up and Bennington clicks excitedly down the hallway to the living room, still barking. I stumble along behind.

Yawning, I open the door just a crack. Eve is standing on the porch, looking like a page from *Vanity Fair* in pleated cotton pants and a blouse of morning-glory blue.

"Sunny, I think we should talk," she says.

All at once I am very awake and awash in yesterday's tempestuous events.

"Oh," I say eloquently. I open the door to let her in, realizing that Eve has never even seen my apartment before.

She has brought along a couple of coffees in a paper sack. She reaches in and hands me one.

"I want to apologize for what happened," she begins, for probably the twentieth time since we left the hospital yesterday.

Taking the coffee, I'm seeing myself through her eyes: a groggy, riot-haired girl standing before her in a ripped, baggy t-shirt and panties, a bandage over one eye, and too befuddled even to extend the customary "thank you" or "have a seat."

"Er, let's go into the kitchen," I suggest.

Her Italian sandals clacking 2/4 time on the hardwood floors, Eve does a quick inventory and remarks what a darling place I have.

In the kitchen, I reach into the refrigerator, hunting milk for her coffee. When I turn back around, Eve touches the bandage that covers my shaved brow and the row of seven stitches.

"I'm truly sorry," she says, and a look of worry clouds her fine, clear features as she takes me in her arms, pulling me close. She holds me like this for so long I start to feel faint, and then realize I've been holding my breath.

Light pours in through the windows. We sit facing each other at the breakfast nook, crisscross threads of sun marking our faces and hands. The clear glass bell that hangs from the eaves chimes a fragile note in the breeze, its reflection a blinding spear moving back and forth across our vision.

"This isn't going to be pleasant," she sighs, and her hands tremble a little as her dazzling smile fades. "But it's something you should know."

And Eve warns me that the story she is about to tell is going to change me, and the way that I think of her, and the parts of me and the parts of her that merge to make a friendship; like the motion of waves on sand, adding to, taking away, smoothing out, persevering.

Eve is HIV positive. She says this in the same tone as if saying her eyes are blue, or her hair chestnut brown, or her shoes size seven.

No, Diane was never exposed. It happened after.

"I'll spare you the lurid details," she says. "We got along beautifully for several years, then I don't know, I suppose maybe she got bored. But she wasn't very discreet with her affairs and I started spending more and more time with the people at work. With David, especially."

Eve and David took advantage of discount packages

available to them as travel agents and spent many lost weekends in resort towns. Recreational drugs were plentiful.

"Yeah, coke, heroin, anything to dull the pain of losing Diane," says Eve, recalling how easily she and David gave themselves up to strangers, in bars or at parties, so wasted it almost didn't matter who.

"Diane and I were finished. I'd moved out by then, and for a year I never drew a sober breath. It was insane. Then, David started missing work. I thought at first it was just general dissipation. But then he got to where he was too exhausted to get out of bed anymore. You know.

"And then a lot of other shit happened. I wrecked my car and got thrown in the hospital and they found out I was an IV drug user, which really thrilled Dad. And that's how I lost my job and wound up in rehab.

"So then nobody would hire me. I ended up moving back in over at Diane's and she supported me for about six months. Dad helped me get my place and start the business. He gave me the car.

"David was a little better by this time, too. Some days he'd feel well enough to come over and lie on the divan while I worked. He gave me the incentive to get back on my feet again...before he died."

Looking up from my coffee to her sapphire eyes, I see they are filled with tears. The air rings with a very loud silence. I reach for her hand. It is shaking. I reach for her other hand. I get up from the table and stand beside her, hands on either side of her face.

"I just couldn't stand the thought of Diane having you." Her voice cracks. She looks away.

I stroke her hair as if she could read my thoughts through my fingertips, and I hold her—the warmth of her skin, the scent of her breath, the beat of her heart like a wordless song in my hands.

☾ ☾ ☾

It is Monday, and my morning coffee waits on the table when I walk in. Eve's playing back all her phone messages and the beeps appear to be annoying Olga, who's sulking, her important nap interrupted. I recognize the soft, low resonance of Diane's voice.

"Hey, Pussy," she says. That's her name for Eve. "Hey, Pussy, there's a get-together out at Suzanne and Snappy Pat's Tuesday night, some kind of a psychic group. I think the three of us should go. So let me know if you can make it."

Diane has always possessed a strong interest in psychic phenomena. Several years ago, as a reporter for the *Renfield Journal*, she won an award for her investigative series on werewolves, UFOs, and ghost-sightings. Only Diane could pull something like that off.

We go in Diane's Jeep. Pat and Suzanne's A-frame cabin is about sixteen miles outside of town on a steep and winding road. It's dark when we get there and we're greeted by a chorus of tree frogs everywhere at once. There are five other cars in the gravel drive, but in the moonlight they all look blue or silver, and the only one I recognize is Pat's pickup.

Suzanne meets us at the door, makes introductions. A couple of the women I have seen before, one named Sweet Jane, and a local artist named Bev. The others are from different towns or out-of-state, and they're all watching a video of *Three Men And a Baby*, which strikes me as a little unusual until Suzanne explains that supposedly there's a ghost in one scene; not part of the movie, but a real ghost. Everyone gets excited when the little boy behind the curtain makes his appearance. Someone rewinds it; there he is again. Ghost or not, he give me the willies.

The mood of the evening having been established, the conversation now turns to the flurry of nearby UFO sightings in the area. There's a front-page story about it in one of the local papers, and Pat relates an account of strange glowing lights and peculiar noises back in the woods that spook the animals.

We watch another video about Hopi Indian prophecies and are shown a map of what the continental United States might look like in the very near future. Much of it is under water. The narrator tells us our lives are becoming so compressed and accelerated that our thought-forms manifest themselves instantaneously, and advises us to be careful of what we think about and what we ask for.

When the tape's finished, Suzanne passes around a platter of freshly baked brownies and we sprawl around talking and drinking coffee. Sweet Jane comes over and sits down on the floor beside the couch and says she couldn't help noticing the bond between Eve, Diane and me. She says it's a very strong one.

The three of us look at each other, and then back at Jane.

"If you'd be interested in pursuing it, maybe we could do a hypnotic regression sometime," she suggests, and gives me her business card.

It's very late when we leave. The night is black and the gravel road is filled with twists and turns. The Jeep's headlights seem inadequate. As we are nearing town, Diane explains about hypnotic regression.

"It's an altered state," she says, "that can enable you to go back in time and reexperience past-life events."

Eve blows a thin cloud of smoke out the window. "I don't believe in any of that crap," she says flatly.

"What about you, Sunny?" Diane asks, turning to where I sit cross-legged in back.

"Anything's possible, I guess," I reply, noncommittal.

But the rest of the way home I ponder in uneasy silence Jane's remark about the bond between Eve, Diane and me.

☾ ☾ ☾

It is Thursday evening and we've just finished a fabulous dinner at Diane's, compliments of Eve. She fixes egg-drop soup, wonton, and shrimp stir fry, and for dessert, there's tropical fruit salad and fortune cookies. My cookie says:

MANY GEISHA GIRL COME TO YOUR HOUSE VERY NEAR FUTURE

Eve and Diane are trying hard not to laugh.

"Am I correct in suspecting a little sabotage here?" I ask.

Diane ignores me and chats enthusiastically about the career potential in fortune-cookie writing. Eve suggests we all collaborate, with her baking the cookies and Diane and me doing the fortunes. It's a must for a New Year's party, they decide.

I'm still at the table and Eve's at the sink rinsing dishes. She's wearing a chef's striped apron that says, "Life is uncertain, eat dessert first!" Diane comes up behind her, they're having a conversation, and as though she's done it hundreds of times before, without thinking, she puts her arms around Eve, hugs her from behind. She leans her head on Eve's shoulder for just a second, and I see Eve sort of arching her back so that her butt nestles against the front of Diane's thighs.

The comfortableness of the gesture somehow makes me feel like an intruder, but just as quickly as it begins, it's over, and Diane has opened the refrigerator to put something away and they're still talking.

Later, as the three of us are sitting in the study and Diane is reading to us from an old Oriental horoscope paperback she found at a garage sale, I get this sudden, outrageous image of the two of them in an intimate embrace. It's so vivid I blush. Where did it come from? I don't know. Maybe I've tapped into the house's cellular memory.

They are lying in bed. Eve is stretched out beneath Diane, her dark hair flung across a satin pillow. I can see her breasts and the sharp lines of her hips as she moves, tense, eyes closed, lips apart. Diane leans close, whispering. I can almost hear her words. In the simple, ravishing music of her hurry she lunges into Eve, their bodies moving as one. Eve's legs arch gracefully up and over Diane. She buries herself in her lover's neck. There is an interminable wait.

The image comes so fast and hard it takes my breath away, and for several seconds I would give anything to have been Diane.

It suddenly feels awfully hot in here to me. Diane drones on about the Chinese zodiac, telling Eve she's born the year of the Snake, Diane is a Monkey, and I am a Dragon.

I get up to go to the bathroom.

When I come back, Diane has put the book aside and is letting Eve massage her temples. I stand in the doorway for several moments watching the look of dark concentration on Eve's face, and the look of childlike peace on Diane's. Waves of old familiar love seem to rise from them like steam.

☾ ☾ ☾

Snappy Pat's Small Engine Repair is a tiny shop in the alley off 9th Street where Pat can usually be found tinkering when she's not tending bar or orchestrating drug deals. Tonight, Bennington and I drop by to chat because I'm feeling a little low and being around Pat always cheers me up. Over in the corner of her shop a charred, greasy radio is squawking out a Patsy Cline tune.

Pat's doing a lot of cussing and gets irate when Bennington runs off with a spark plug. She tells me Kristy and Marie have broken up, again, and that the back porch blew off Maxine's house during that squall we had two nights ago.

"Oh," I reply.

Other tidbits: Misty and Pam want a child, Laine finally got tenure, Andrea's house is up for sale, Jones got another speeding ticket, Billie's Burmese cat just had kittens.

☾ ☾ ☾

I miss Kim. I need to tell her face-to-face what is happening. My mind roams back to our first meeting.

When I moved here to Renfield for my first year of college, I had trouble finding a place that was affordable, close to campus, and that allowed pets. So when I found this apartment on the ground floor of an elegant Victorian house on Kentucky Street, I took it, even though it wasn't affordable. And I began looking around frantically for a roommate.

This was easier said than done. I wasn't prepared for the onslaught of calls in response to my tiny ad in the paper. It was scary. One woman, who'd just been released from prison, drove a pickup across my front lawn, killing my impatiens ("Is it okay to park here?") and said she thought by nonsmoker I'd meant someone who didn't do crack or pot. "Yeah, I'm clean," she brayed, slipping a Chesterfield from her pack.

Three blonde juveniles came up one morning, possibly cheerleaders, possibly clones, probably Tri-Deltas. They had paper-shredder hair and spoke very fast in high, jerky voices, as if vibrator abuse had short-circuited their brains. I was nervous for the rest of the day.

My next caller was a man scheduled for sex-change surgery who thought it would be ever so divine having a woman roommate to, you know, show him the ropes while he made the transition. I said I didn't think so.

So when Kim showed up at my door looking like a plundering, ransacking pirate, you have to understand it was a rather titillating, thrilling contrast to some of the people I'd talked to.

I say pirate because of the large gold hoop in one ear and the red bandanna. Those two things alone might not have made such an impression, had it not been for the eye patch. I half-expected her to strike a match on the seat of her pants.

"Hello," I said. "I'm Sunny Calhoun. Come on in."

"Kim," she nodded.

I found I was liking her before we even made it to the kitchen. It was the slow, deliberate way she appraised things, and the graceful way she moved, and how she looked me in the eye when she spoke.

I took her through the light-filled living room explaining that any improvements we made, such as installing shades or mini-blinds, would be deducted from the rent. And although there was no carpet, the landlord seemed willing enough to provide it, but actually I preferred the look and feel of wood floors, and so did she.

"Here's the dining room," I said, pointing out that the southern exposure would be ideal for plants, "and here are the kitchen and bath, both huge, the way they used to make them back when this house was built."

I showed her both bedrooms, situated on either side of the bathroom.

"I like it," she said.

As we sat at the table negotiating terms, Kim revealed that her eye patch was temporary, the result of a softball mishap.

She moved in the next day, and over the past three years we've become best of friends. More than that, Kim has become my rock. I've been spoiled by her stability, her companionship, and never has it been more evident than now.

Now that she's away on this summer internship, I feel lost. I miss her bike on the porch next to mine. I miss the sweet, aromatic fragrances of her perfumes and bubble baths. I miss the unself-conscious melody of her singing, and the sensual, sometimes lusty roar of laughter as she talks on the phone with friends.

I miss her teasing when I take myself too seriously, winking and saying, "Redheads are so dumb!"

I call her tonight for the second time in a week.

"Sunny!" she says, answering the phone. "Sunny Bo-Bunny, Bo-nana mana fo-funny, fee fie fo money, Sunny...Hey, what's up, girl?"

"Oh, nothing much."

"Woa, you sound kinda tore down."

"It's Eve."

"Eve? Now what? She fire you?"

"No, no."

"Oh. Well hang on then, let me switch phones."

I can hear her grandma laughing at something on TV and then Kim picks up the extension in her room, and there's a click as someone hangs up and Kim says, "Okay, I'm back. And you know what, I think Eve is messing with your mind."

"No, I don't think so."

"Right. You're just so in love you don't see it."

"I'm not in love!"

"Excuse me. You're not in love."

"I'm just confused, Kim. I haven't felt this way about anyone since Annie."

"Then go for it."

"That's just it. I can't."

"Why?"

"Well, because it's such a mixed-up situation. I think she and Diane are still in love."

"Hmmmm. Is Eve still flirting with you?"

"Yes."

"Then listen. Call her bluff."

"What do you mean?"

"The next time she pulls you down on that bed of hers all drunk and wanting a hug, or a kiss, or a good-night story, call her bluff. Sounds to me like Eve only wants what she thinks she can't have. I know the type."

"No. You're wrong. Not Eve."

"Suit yourself. Just give her a little taste, Sunny. Let her know two can play that game."

Kim's wrong, I decide, after we've hung up. What Eve

really wants is to make Diane jealous. She's using me to try and get back at her.

But nah. I can't believe Eve would do such a thing. She's much more aware than most people. I should know, I work with her every day. Kim has misjudged Eve. She doesn't know her, hasn't even met her. Eve's just Eve. A little wild, a little unorthodox, a little self-destructive maybe, but basically good-hearted and kind.

All at once I realize that, like myself, Eve is very lonely.

☾ ☾ ☾

All morning it has rained. I wake to the squish of wet tires passing on the street by my house, and think of an old friend who says rain can be one of two things. When life is good, it means the angels are washing their hair. When it's bad, they're crying. Today, then, a shampoo waterfall outside my open window.

It is Sunday and the choir from the Full Gospel Assembly down at the corner sweetens the air with hymns. Bennington clicks from room to room as I sit having coffee in my big white kitchen.

There's no sign of Diane's Jeep across the alley. I wonder if she might have gone home with Eve after the barbecue out at Pat and Suzanne's last night. An image comes to mind of the two of them sprawled in Eve's shiny brass bed, disorderly, sheets tangled like crepe paper. Diane is naked on her tummy with an arm flung over Eve, who's on her side, half-dressed, with ashtrays and tipped-over Heineken bottles strewn all over the floor and nightstand. I dismiss it quickly, wondering who all ended up staying out at the cabin after the housewarming party broke up.

As housewarming celebrations go, it was okay. Things were fairly subdued when I caught a ride back to town after midnight. The cabin was an A-frame with a hot-tub out on the deck, and it was pleasant to lounge out there hearing tree frogs, gazing up at the sky. Jones and I counted five shooting stars and as many UFOs.

I talked to a visiting couple from Chattanooga, one of them a writer, who kept brushing her arm against my breasts and telling me how much I looked like Shirley MacLaine.

There was supposed to have been a band there, too, but Snappy Pat told us the lead singer was thrown from her Harley the night before, and the drummer, who was with her, broke an arm, so they had to cancel.

Between fifty and sixty guests showed up, and gifts ranged from a dulcimer, hand made by some of the mountain women living on a co-op several towns away, to pottery, artwork, handmade clothing, homemade bread and pastries, a few jugs of Patty Euphoria's famous Thunderberry wine, a giant cactus, a shower curtain, hand-dipped candles, crystals, gemstones, a slightly dented washer and dryer, five pounds of pecans, a large chunk of petrified wood, and all manner of decorative lawn ornaments, including pink flamingos, ladybugs, dinosaurs, and tarantulas. Diane, Eve and I went in together on a Black Forest cuckoo clock from the downtown thrift store. Somehow, it seemed like just the thing, and turned out to be a tremendous hit.

5

Mom calls, wanting to know if I'll be flying home for the Fourth of July or what. I tell her Snappy Pat's got a rebuilt VW bug down at the shop she'll loan me for the trip. Fine, then. Will you be bringing anyone with you? I don't think so, Mom. Will you need some money? No Mom, thanks.

"Tell your friend Eve she's more than welcome."

"I'll tell her, Mom, but I think she has plans."

Actually, I'm looking forward to a few days away from Eve. Lately it seems like all I've done is fantasize about her. Just once I wish she'd let go of that cool exterior and do something totally out of character. Like assault me. Forcibly. Again and again.

I get a little paranoid worrying that somehow she's aware of when I'm thinking, um, impure thoughts about her. But sometimes during the day she'll run her hand across my shoulders, or brush against my thigh, or I'll catch her looking at me a certain way and I wonder if she's having similar thoughts about me.

"—be expecting you around suppertime, then. What about Diane? Does she have plans?"

Mom's a big fan of Diane's, owns autographed copies of all her books. Mom herself is a writer who leans toward philosophy. When she came to stay with me last summer, she and Diane would hole up over at Diane's for entire afternoons, reading and talking. I'd come home from my job at the library and find them sitting around discussing parallel galaxies and ninth-dimensional fluctuations, or the similarities between canzones and sestinas. Other times they might be doing crystal meditations or aura purification exercises. I never knew what to expect. But then, with my mother, I have learned that one must be prepared for anything.

Mother used to embarrass me all the time when I was growing up. Like the time she decided to shave her head. It was right after she quit her job as a letter carrier for the post office, and on the advice of a psychic, she and Dad started up the bed-and-breakfast. Duke and Katherine are ex-flower children and they're extremely nuts. I used to think my brother Jim and I were a huge disappointment to them because we're so nauseatingly conservative by their standards.

Even my grandmother on Mom's side is an old hippie. She and Aunt Buck (not really an aunt at all) owned the greenhouse where Dad worked when he was between professions, which was most of the time. When Mom started lamenting that all Dad did was loaf around reading poetry, Grandma Malone got the bright idea of putting him back to work. This was right after Aunt Buck's assertiveness training workshop when she got a little carried away and broke her foreman's nose. So Dad took his job.

Aunt Buck's real name is Marie Buckingham. She and Grandma have been together nearly twenty years now. When I was little sometimes I'd refer to Grandma as Aunt Buck's wife and it really confused my teachers.

"—and Dad's got your old room just packed with books he thinks you might like," Mom is saying.

"Great," I remark. They've been running a used-book store for several years now. It's been surprisingly successful.

"Drive carefully, baby."

"I will, Mom."

"We'll see you day after tomorrow, then. I love you."

"I love you, too, Mom."

☾ ☾ ☾

The bug that Snappy Pat loans me is flaming sunset orange with extra wide tires, deep tinted windows, and a sunroof. She's asking $2,400 for it. I stop by Eve's on Wednesday morning to show it off on my way out of town.

"Cute," she says. "Are you going to buy it?"

"It's tempting," I say. "But what I really want is a van. For camping. And vision-quests."

Eve smiles. "Yeah, that would suit you. The roving poet and her bed on wheels." She takes a crisp green bill from her robe and tucks it deep into the pocket of my shorts.

"Lunch money," she says. She leans over suddenly, taking my chin in her hands, and kisses me, hard, on the mouth. "Drive carefully, kiddo."

I can't resist. I lean over, take her chin in my hands, look her in the eye, and say, "I will."

The trip home takes about eight hours. It's a fairly uneventful cruise until the tape player starts eating my tapes. The radio's broken, so to pass the time I accuse Bennington of shape-shifting. She wakes from her nap and looks around hopefully. She looks quite sly wearing her freshly laundered red bandanna. When I begin singing to her, she flops down with a heavy sigh and puts her paws over her ears. Unappreciative degenerate.

I chug along on autopilot, thinking back to my conversation with Kim last night. What I can remember of it, that is. She woke me around 2 a.m. all in an uproar over Celia. "Oh, she's so talented, so fabulous, omigod, Sunny, so, so incredibly, so absolutely, devastatingly, totally, and she's, for example, *really* into poetry Sunny, so can you like make some suggestions, name some names, give me an idea where to start...?"

"Ummm, ummm," I say, trying hard to wake up.

"—okay, there's this one she mentioned at dinner, uh, Olga something, she's Greek and extremely oh, what was it"

"Wait," I interrupt. "Olga Broumas?"

"Yes! That's it!"

"Cool. So you and Celia had dinner, eh?"

"—really far out place called The Island. Sunny you'd have loved it. We ended up working real late, see, and—"

I keep nodding off in my pillow, then waking with a start to Kim's full-blast chatter.

"—said something about fly up to San Francisco over the weekend. It'd be Dana and Toni and her ex—"

This is so unlike my cool, discerning Kim, my inscrutable Virgo companion on whom I've relied for so long—her flawless logic, her legendary reserve now shattered...

Celia's her boss. Kim's in love with her boss. Can you believe it?

☾ ☾ ☾

It's nearly six o'clock by the time I exit the freeway onto County Road 9 that will take me to my parents' house. Within minutes I'm headed into woods that lead down a twisting road to Bush Lake, and I'm smelling fireworks as I speed through the old neighborhood waving at the Merediths and the Olsons who are out tossing firecrackers around on their lawn. I think I can even smell the barbecue sauce as I thunder up Pickfair Drive and round the last curve to Mom and Dad's. Finally, here we are, wheeling into the circle drive, honking and barking, and there's Mom on the porch watering her geraniums...

The first thing out of her mouth when I step from the car is, "Sunny, What On Earth Has Happened To Your Forehead?"

"Hi, Mom. I uh, slid on a beer can and fell off my bike?" I grin. She wraps her arms around me and I get one of those we'll-talk-about-this-later looks. Dad appears in his chef's apron, twirling a spatula. We hug. Grandma and Aunt Buck come dashing around the side of the house wearing matching capri pants and loud t-shirts. Grandma's is Easter-egg blue and says "Discover Greater Miami Opera!"

"Oh, how lovely!" she says, meaning my car. "Can I have a ride?"

"You mean you drove all the way from Renfield in that *dune buggy*?" croaks Aunt Buck in disbelief. As we take turns hugging, the screen door flies open and Jim pops out like a jack-in-the-box and Bennington starts jumping up and down, yapping wildly at whatever he's holding in his arms. A baby kangaroo? Everyone's talking at once.

My brother looks a lot like Tom Cruise. He'll be a senior in high school this fall, and unlike me, has always known exactly what he wants to be when he grows up. He's working for Dad's golf buddy Hugh Rivard this summer, feeding and caring for pets, appeasing clients, and attending to the numerous other general assistance duties performed by veterinarian flunkies. The kangaroo that he has brought home from work is named Edith. She boings behind on spring-loaded haunches wherever he goes.

Bennington (who was my brother's bon voyage gift to me the week I left for college) seems positively enamored of Edith. If she were able to remove her scarf and present it as a love offering, I think she would.

☾ ☾ ☾

As always, an odd and interesting assortment of characters have assembled at my parent's Fourth of July party.

The first to arrive is Grandma's friend Faye, a mezzo-soprano. Faye is in town for a convention and greets Grandma at the front door with a resonant, tremoring, operatic bellow, which Grandma attempts to duplicate. Melrose shoots under the divan. Quite unceremoniously, Faye thwacks her way over the flagstone entryway with an ornate hickory walking stick, complaining every step of the way of car rental agencies, denouncing the airlines, griping about her dentures, demanding a glass of wine. She hasn't changed much since the last time I saw her, except her hair is even shorter, and she's gotten new glasses, huge black stellar things that make her look like Roy Orbison. A real '90s kinda gal, as Grandma likes to say.

Mom and Dad are upstairs getting ready. Jim and I are arranging the hors d'oeuvres, when Lola Macy sweeps in with a floral arrangement, a centerpiece of red, white, and blue carnations. Dad comes downstairs, barefoot and shirtless, wondering if he has any clean socks in the dryer.

"Yes," Jim hollers. "I just did a load of underthings this morning."

Shrieks of laughter drift in from the patio. The doorbell rings, Lola goes to answer it. Dad disappears into the laundry room. Mom appears, looking casual in loose white cotton pants and a blue shirt, her hair braided. She wears no makeup except lipstick, and has on the gold hummingbird earrings I gave her for Christmas.

"Cool, Mom," I say.

Soon the house fills. Night falls. Some of the neighbor kids are out in boats making firework displays on the water. Guests are milling around on the patio, the deck, out in the yard.

When Mom introduces me to a special friend of hers from Berkeley, I'm feeling quite chatty and informative. She's a science-fiction writer. Her name is Marion Zimmer Bradley. I also meet several performance artists, a composer, a tuba virtuoso, a Supreme Court Justice, the CEO of Loose Orchestra Enterprises, a geologist, a spy, and a gifted conversationalist named Loii from the planet of the Red Sun.

Terry Amberg drops by after midnight, and we make a polite sweep through the house, patio and yard, so she can say hi to everyone, which takes about twenty minutes. Then we cross the street to her parents. Sparklers and roman candles are lighting up the whole block.

When we were eleven, Terry and I vowed our eternal

love for each other. In the woods behind her house, we performed an elaborate ritual involving pricking our fingers and mixing our blood. This made us soul sisters, she said.

Growing older, I'm finding that love isn't always this simple and pure, but never, ever has it touched me as deeply, or rubbed its sweet, shiny hands all over me so thoroughly.

It feels so good to be home.

☾ ☾ ☾

It's very late, and Grandma is plying me with her Highland whiskey.

"Does your girlfriend beat you, dear?" she finally asks in hushed tones of alarm, lightly touching my brow.

"Heavens, no," I slur. "I don't even have a girlfriend."

"That's quite a nasty cut, sweetheart. Would you like to tell me how it happened?"

"Yes, I would, but not now, Grandma. I just want to go to bed."

I stumble down the hall and up the stairs to my old room, which now contains a lot of overflow from the bookstore, along with selections Dad doesn't want to part with. The room is a gold mine. I could hibernate in here for weeks. Dad has even started a box for me with items he thinks I might like.

Something by Hayden Carruth catches my eye, and something by Elizabeth Bishop...Stanley Kunitz...Mary Oliver woa! Excellent choice, Dad. I'm going through this box first thing in the morning. But for now, it's 2 a.m., and everyone else is in bed and I'm so tired I can't think. As I pull back the sheet and kick off my shorts, something falls out of the pocket. I stoop to pick it up. Lunch money. Eve. A hundred dollar bill.

☾ ☾ ☾

When I wake at sunrise the house is very still. A fernlike glaze of sun sprays through my louvered windows, decorating the floor and bed with lacy plumes of golden silk. Somewhere off in the trees a woodpecker starts its day by drilling and pounding, banging its head against a tree trunk.

Bennington gets up from her rug and stretches as I pull on my shirt and shorts. We slip down the hall, inhaling the cedar and spice and dried eucalyptus that I never really notice until I've been gone. Light shimmers through the kitchen and living room windows. I creep barefoot down the stairs, surprised at the softness, realizing Mom has recarpeted in a shade of soft wintergreen.

Dad's aging Burmese cat, Melrose, is snoozing on top of the TV as we make our way through the sliding glass door which has been left open all night. Bennington and I exit onto the deck, littered with remains of last night's dinner. The Macys and Hendersons were here; empty beer cans and ashtrays mark their spots. I see Lola Macy has left her gold lighter.

Crossing the back yard to the lake, I hear the loon in the distance, rattling my nerves with its cry. The sun through the trees paints a bleeding copper-pink across the water. Mist rises from its center and from nearby marshy patches of cattails and reeds lined with birds along the shore.

The water is very cool on my feet, the sandy bottom squishes between my toes. Bennington plunges in wildly, pursuing a duck. I untie the scarred, battered paddleboat at the dock and push off into the glassy water, Bennington splashing behind, her scarf now floating on the silky surface.

I paddle into deep water, the flat sides of the runners making loud thwacking sounds. Bennington swims ashore, shakes herself. She stares after me curiously, ears cocked. Behind her on the embankment is our house, its weathered cedar walls shadowed beneath oak and spruce and pine.

Halfway across the lake I stand up in the boat and

breathe the morning air. I pull off my clothes and jackknife into the water, swimming on my back in lazy circles. The sky is white and hot-looking.

There is a song I once played over and over because it embodied so perfectly the mood of a piece I was trying to write. I wish I could do that now—sustain the feeling of being suspended in time, that same magical sensation you get when you've just seen a really good play and you walk out of the theatre and anything, anything is possible...that altered state where you're so tightly woven into the fabric of the moment that you're beyond caring whether you can recreate it some other time or not...

☾ ☾ ☾

An hour later I'm back in the kitchen fixing breakfast, hearing Grandma and Aunt Buck squabble over something down the hall in the room they're using while their condo is being restored. A police helicopter crashed into the side of their building last month and the entire east wing had to be evacuated until repairs could be made. I know it sounds silly, but that's what happened. And since they both tend to be rather short-tempered, it doesn't surprise me that the novelty of their new and temporary housing arrangement is starting to wear off.

I hear a loud thud, the kind that sounds like a frying pan hitting the wall, followed by cursing and exclamations. Their door flies open and Grandma stomps out, bristling, and comes pounding stiff-legged into the kitchen. She looks ready to eat bricks. Her snowy white hair sticks out in front like antlers, and is plastered to her head on the sides, while the back is dripping wet.

"Cool hairdo," I say. "You and Aunt Buck have a water fight, Grandma?"

She mutters something unintelligible. She's wearing the cutest little pajamas, blue and white dotted Swiss with tiny dancing giraffes. She keeps up a lively diatribe under her breath while pouring coffee, and when the phone rings she answers it abruptly.

"Hello," she barks. "Yes...yes...I see...yes, she's here, just a moment...Sunny, it's that girlfriend of yours," she says darkly. "Wants to know why you didn't show up for work."

I lunge for the phone.

"EVE?"

"Hi, kiddo."

"Hi!" My heart is singing.

"You okay?"

"Yeah, I'm fine. How're you?"

"Fine. Just wanted to make sure you got there safely."

"Oh, yeah, uneventful trip, no problems."

"Good, good. Everything all right?"

"Fine, fine. Oh, and thanks for the lunch money."

"No big deal. You've earned it."

"Well, thanks."

"Family glad to see you?"

"Yeah."

"Hope I didn't wake anyone."

"You didn't. We're up. I went swimming in the lake."

"Sounds lovely."

"Oh, it was. Beautiful. Like a dream. I wish—"

Pause.

"Yes?"

I wish you were here, I was going to say. "I wish I could describe it..." But I haven't the words.

"Well, it's sure quiet around here without you. Glad you got there safely. Have a great time, kiddo... Don't you dare drown. And be careful coming home."

"Thanks. I will."

Pause.

"Don't have *too* much fun while you're gone."

"Oh, right," I grin.

"I almost forgot, Sunny. A note came in the mail for

you yesterday from *Calyx.* They've accepted your poem."

"Really? Which one?"

"'Orchestra of Blue Music.'"

"Grandma, guess what? Eve's sold one of my poems!"

"Outstanding," says Grandma, brightening somewhat. "Perhaps this tawdry little romance might be leading somewhere after all."

"Grandma! It isn't tawdry!" I hiss.

"Nobody said it was," Eve answers. "I think it's a very good poem. I thought you'd be excited."

"Oh, I am, I am."

"Good. Well, happy Fourth of July, kiddo. Gotta go."

"Thanks for calling, Eve."

"Bye now."

6

It's Monday night and I'm back in Renfield. Eve and I are sitting in her car at the Dairy Queen. I've driven across town to the one on 6th because Eve doesn't like the one on Main, and she likes the old man who runs this one. He has dignity, she says.

I get a Buster bar. Eve gets a Blizzard. It's so sweet it's making her sick. I tell her to save the rest for Bennington, but she keeps on eating.

It's about closing time. We sit in the parking lot as cars continue piling to the drive-thru window. We're beneath a streetlight that hums steadily. Insects are flying around. A shiny black pickup rolls by, speakers blaring, bass rattling our windshield. The red and blue neon light from the OPEN sign reflects in the rear view mirror, blinking on and off, on and off, on and off. Above us there's a strange line of clouds filling the sky from the north, turning it black, moving closer.

Eve reaches over to put a CD into the player but it slips out of her fingers and rolls to the floor by my feet. We bend to pick it up and practically clonk heads.

A shiver runs through me as I catch the light, dry scent of Eve's skin and hair, inches from my lips. She pauses, as if aware of my thoughts. The CD remains where it has fallen, as slowly, transfixed, we sit upright in our seats. Eve's eyes seem to sparkle. Eve's eyes seem to shine. From off in the distance comes the rumble of thunder.

☾ ☾ ☾

There's a patio on the roof at Eve's that looks out over her back yard and is shaded by elms and maples for most of the morning. Weeks ago Eve had dragged a black wrought-iron table with a glass top up there, and topped it with a frayed umbrella. Then came a barbecue grill and some deck chairs.

This morning Eve decides to have brunch out here. She bakes some caramel-pecan rolls and calls me up and I come over and we fill Bavarian crystal goblets with sliced fruit. Diane brings a container of orange juice and we feast. Later, the two of them drink coffee and read the Sunday paper while I lie back listening to the headphones.

Some time after noon Eve goes inside and comes back carrying drinks on a tray. They're piña coladas in hollowed-out coconut shells, complete with green and lilac paper umbrellas and fruit slices speared on little plastic swords.

After a few of these we stretch out in the sun and Diane and Eve gossip about an assistant curator Eve has been doing some work for. She's fun and articulate, says Eve, but she finds her sly innuendos revolting, and when she suggests they go away together for the weekend, Eve always tells her she can't, she's just too busy.

"I can just picture it," Eve giggles. "She'd be worse than a guy." She winks and leers. "Why, she'd even be worse than you."

"You wish," says Diane, and whispers something, and Eve whispers back, and they shriek, tipsy, feeling no pain.

"Or," says Eve, "something kinky like making me read *Paris Match* out loud to her while she ea-"

"Excuuuuuuse me, girls?" I say loudly, clearing my throat.

"Why, Eve, I believe she's blushing," says Diane.

"Put your headphones back on, kiddo."

"You're supposed to be working on your tan, not Evesdropping," Diane chides with a giggle.

Eve reaches over mischievously and yanks my tube top down around my waist.

"Oh, dear God," she says in mock alarm, "little Muffy is starting to get breasts!"

I yank my top back up.

"Breasts indeed," chimes Diane. "Perhaps it's time we divulge to her the facts of life."

"And pack her off to a proper finishing school to find out for herself."

"Yes, yes. Something along the line of Miss Edna's?"

"Splendid choice. As you know, I spent fourteen lovely years there myself. Great fun."

They chitter and crack up.

"Muffy darling, would you mind securing another round of drinks?"

"Eve dearest, I suspect our young charge is too overcome to curtsy, much less manage drinks."

"Quite so. I shall summon Percival at once."

Diane gets up from her lawn chair, loses her balance, and lands with a crash in Eve's lap.

"Lord have mercy," I mutter, looking skyward.

Eve's chair collapses beneath the sudden impact. Thrashing and laughing, they flounder against each other, heaving with spasms of hysteria, tears in their eyes as the two of them lie in a drunken, joyous, tangled heap.

I reach over to help Diane to her feet, wishing it were me, and not her, in Eve's arms.

☾ ☾ ☾

A letter and a small check arrive in the mail. Eve tells me three of my poems have been accepted by a little magazine called *New Avenue.* I didn't even know she had been sending them out. I don't know what to do so I just smile, and to celebrate I take Eve and

Diane out to dinner and we take turns feeding each other dessert.

☾ ☾ ☾

Several days later as I'm driving around downtown, looking for a parking place near the office supply store where Eve has sent me on an errand, I spot Sweet Jane across the street. It would be hard to miss her in that flowered skirt and amethyst-colored blouse. She's loping along on the cobblestones rather unsteadily in Birkenstocks, and her wheat-colored hair, tied in a lavender scarf, gleams in the morning sun like polished brass.

I toot the horn and wave. Sweet Jane glances up, doesn't recognize Eve's Mercedes, and puts her hand over her eyes to block the sun, staring. A truck lurches away from a parking space beside her and I do a U-turn to snag it, rolling up alongside Jane, who's still staring. She recognizes me and comes around to the driver's side of the car and tells me she's glad to see me because I've been on her mind since the meeting out at Snappy Pat's and would I have time for lunch?

Well, sure. I lock the car, feed quarters into the meter, and we veer up the steep street towards the Hop. As we're being seated in the bustling sidewalk cafe, Jane tells me one of her missions for the day is to find some pennyroyal for her dog Morris. It repels fleas and insects, she says. Jane's been living in her camper out in the wilds all summer, working on her art. I saw some of her basketwork in a gallery on Spring Street last week. The price was staggering.

I order a turkey sandwich and Jane orders a hamburger. The waiter brings our tea and Jane lights a Pall Mall. I excuse myself to call Eve to see if she'd like me to bring her anything for lunch.

She answers on about the eighth ring.

"Where the hell are you?" she barks. "The Hop? What're you doing there?"

"I ran into Sweet Jane."

"Oh, God. That psycho?"

"Do you want anything or not?"

"Yes. I want you back here. It's a zoo."

Her attitude is really starting to annoy me.

"Bring me a chicken sandwich," she says, "with barbecue sauce. And some curly fries. And watch yourself, kiddo. She's after something."

Eve's so paranoid. When I return to our table, Sweet Jane is stabbing out her cigarette and smiling.

"Eve doesn't like me very much, does she?"

I must look rattled, because her smile broadens.

"It's okay," she says, with a wink. "I know. She's just trying to protect her little sweetie from the big bad witch."

I just stare at Jane dumbly.

She laughs. "It's pretty obvious how much Eve cares about you, and there's a definite psychic bond between the three of you."

"You talking about Diane?"

She nods as the waiter brings our food.

As we're eating, Jane mentions she's leaving for Santa Fe in another week or so. She seldom spends more than a couple of months in any one location, and there's an art show coming up she's preparing for. But before she goes, she says, she'd like to do a past-life regression on me. Free of charge.

I'm interested, but a little curious. I can't help wondering about her motives.

"Why me?" I ask.

"Call it a hunch," comes her mysterious reply.

"Something in my aura?" I ask hopefully.

There is a pause. "Frankly, Sunny, I don't see auras." There is an even longer pause. "I prefer to look beneath the surface."

We finish our meal in silence. As we're leaving the restaurant, I tell her yes, I would indeed be interested in having a past-life regression.

"Good," she says, smiling. "How about this evening?"

"Fine," I reply. "I'll be there."

Eve says nothing when I walk into the house. She pretends to be overwhelmingly occupied with a document she's composing on the computer. I walk over and plunk the lunch sack down beside her.

"Well?" she says suddenly.

I walk away. "Well what?"

How I love it when those blue eyes flash.

"What did she want, Sunny?"

"She doesn't *want* anything, Eve," I sigh. "She's just going to do an age regression on me to find out past-life stuff. I think it'll be fun."

"She's *what* ?"

I walk out of the room and head for the back office.

"When?" she yells.

"Tonight," I roar.

"Where?"

"Her place."

She's behind me at once. "Oh no you don't. You're not going out in those creepy woods all alone with her."

I turn to face her, really quite exasperated now, but her expression takes me by surprise. I say nothing at all.

"Call her up. Say you're not going."

"I can't. She doesn't have a phone."

"Then don't go."

"I already said I would and I am."

We don't speak for the rest of the afternoon.

☾ ☾ ☾

Diane, Eve and I end up driving out to Sweet Jane's in the Jeep. Since I had planned on borrowing the Jeep to get out there anyway, Eve phoned Diane all in a huff urging her to try and talk me out of going, but Diane knows better than to argue with either one of us, so all three of us going seems to be the simplest solution. Besides, Diane's as curious as I am.

Eve rides along glowering in the back. There's a wall between us at least a foot thick. Diane is chattering above the radio, saying how nice it would be to live away from the city, pointing out the black and gold flash of an oriole, swerving to avoid a raccoon on this backwater road.

Sweet Jane has camped for the summer on the edge of a development that extends far into the hills. As we climb the dark, twisting road an occasional gap in the foliage offers a panoramic view of the rosy sunset fanning bluish hills, and the silver and lilac surface of a lake far below. Diane wants to come back here early some morning with her camera, she says excitedly. Coughing from the dust, Eve growls she doesn't know why anyone would want to live way out here all alone.

I watch her in the rear view mirror. She sulks in the corner behind Diane, her dark hair hanging loose on her shoulders like Alice in Wonderland. She is clearly nervous. As for me, I have never felt more at home.

Wolf Ridge Road ends on the acreage where Jane has parked her little Scotty trailer. She has tapped into the power lines of the owners, who allow her to stay on their property in exchange for watching over their cabin while they vacation in Italy.

Sweet Jane seems pleased that all three of us have shown up. Morris, who appears to be part chow, barks and barks and won't shut up. Jane finally calms him with a couple of chicken wings, and he sullenly slinks behind a cluster of pines.

Jane invites us into her cramped, tiny trailer, which is cluttered with herbs, baskets, beads, feathers, and batches of leather. She offers us wine and we listen to native flute songs while the soft glow of evening fades to black.

A small light burns in the trailer. The night sounds have begun outside—the insects and crickets and unknowns are rocking the trees with their symphony as I lie relaxed on cushions, hearing Jane's soft, insistent voice. I try to concentrate on what she is telling me.

Yes, white light. I see it all around me. All around us. It surrounds the trailer, extending into the gloom beyond the clearing and out into the trees. I seem to be hovering above the treetops. I see Diane's Jeep shining in the windowlight next to Jane's white Impala, and I hear and sense movement back in the trees.

Every part of my body, each cell has become so relaxed that when Sweet Jane tells me I'm floating, it feels like I am. I imagine myself outside my body, and I see the night sky up above. Sweet Jane asks me to describe what I'm seeing. The Big Dipper, I say. The Northern Cross. And a shooting star.

Now Jane suggests that I allow myself to come down slowly and gently to the ground, reminding me that I'm surrounded by white protective light.

I'm drawn to the trees. A strong force pulls me like a magnet and I am looking down at a glowing circle of light unlike anything I have seen before. The light is bronze. But no, it is purple. And green. It pulsates. I am hearing a very high-pitched hum, but also I am hearing Sweet Jane's voice saying Sunny, come away from there, come away now.

I am trying to tell her what I see, but she interrupts, which I find very rude. I would like to stay and watch the pretty lights turning night into day, illuminating the forest, but Jane is becoming impatient with me. All at once I am back on the cushions, in the trailer, with Eve and Diane watching over me, and Sweet Jane is sounding a little tense, and I'm feeling as if I have just been awakened from a very vivid dream.

"Is this normally what happens?" Eve wants to know.

"Not exactly," says Jane. She asks how I feel. Weird but okay. Asks if I want to rest and try it again. Sure, okay. She pours Eve more wine, finds her an ashtray. Morris stands out in the moonlight, howling. Diane keeps glancing out the window toward the trees. The hair is standing up on my arms.

We do it a little differently the second time. If Sweet

Jane has hypnotized me, I'm certainly not aware of it. This time she takes me back further and further behind my childhood, beyond infancy. I recall the luxurious feeling of being in the womb, followed by the feeling of being a 33 rpm record played at 78, except in reverse, as though I'm in a time warp. Streaks of light whiz by. Sounds are distorted. It's like moving around under water and dreaming at the same time. It is not an uncomfortable sensation.

Next, I realize I'm being held. All around is softness and warmth and the close smell of flesh. There is a sweet taste in my mouth. I am incredibly happy. I open my eyes to the light, and see myself at my mother's breast.

I am explaining this to Sweet Jane, but find it tiresome to talk because I am feeling so perfectly content in this woman's arms. I would like to remain here at her breast forever. Jane persists in asking questions.

"Describe the woman."

"She is my mother," I say. "And I already know her."

"What do you mean?"

"I mean she is someone I know."

"Is she your mother in this lifetime also?"

"No," I reply.

"Can you describe her to me?"

I'm becoming impatient with Jane. My mother leans toward me, kissing the fluff on the top of my head, and I recognize those eyes at once, that deep, mottled color of polished tortoise. It is Diane.

"Describe her to me," Jane repeats.

Her hair is braided, dark and long. She is singing to me, and her dark eyes shine in the firelight.

Jane asks me to move forward in time, but that's very difficult to do because I love it where I'm at. She insists. Grudgingly, I comply. But I see nothing. There is only darkness, a void.

"Back up a bit," Jane instructs.

I will myself back, and am once again in my mother's

arms. This time she is bathing me in a clear running brook. Again, she is singing.

"Do you know your mother?" asks Jane.

"Of course."

"How do you know her?"

I pause. Language fails me. Logic fails me. Her hands are caressing my skin, splashing water on my head, down my back.

"I know it is Diane by the way she bathes me," I say.

"Look at yourself. Can you tell if you're female or male?"

"Female."

"Can you tell me about your surroundings?"

I tell her about the great blue and yellow bird that I see beyond the trees. It is the face of a totem pole.

Again, Jane instructs me to move ahead, but when I do, there is harshness. I am freezing, I tell her, trembling. I am too weak to cry out.

"Where is your mother?"

With glazed eyes, I look around through the darkness and gloom. My mother is on the ground beside me. She is not moving. There are snowflakes swirling in a bitter wind and they light on her nose and lips, which are blue.

I flinch and gasp. Sweet Jane asks what is happening, reminds me that I have the power to remove myself from this situation.

"There is a shaggy rug standing over me," I whisper. "And it's blocking the trees, filling the sky."

The rug comes closer. I can smell it. It is not a pleasant smell. With the very last strength that I possess, I wave my arms and shriek as the monster reaches for me.

"What is it?" Diane asks sharply.

The creature is lifting me up, gently, and cradling me close. Two bright eyes burn above a long, black snout.

"It's a grizzly bear," I tell her, stunned.

The bear whines softly. I feel the warmth and roughness of her coat, clutch it with my tiny fingers as she holds me to her with massive paws. A tremor passes through my body, then a feeling of release and joy. There is nothing more.

Silence. Sweet Jane tells me to inhale and exhale slowly, to the count of four. She suggests I imagine myself floating, calmly, in a sea of tranquility for several seconds. She instructs me that when I open my eyes, I will feel rested and whole, and reminds me once again of the white light surrounding all of us, that I am safe and protected.

The first thing that I see in the candlelight is Diane. She's smiling, and there are tears in her eyes. She reaches for my hand. Beside her, Eve is looking a little pale, a little puzzled. She grins at me and winks. Sweet Jane is watching intently.

"Welcome back," she says. "How do you feel?"

"Like I've just been in a very weird movie," I say.

I'm feeling an incredible urge just to hold Diane and cry. Her tawny eyes, always strangely familiar to me somehow, are locked onto mine. A knowing passes between us, too strong for words. In that moment, it is as if a thousand white-winged birds are stirring in our hearts.

☾ ☾ ☾

Diane's in the bathtub with the door open. She's shaving her legs. I'm around the corner in the bedroom helping her pack for a writer's conference in Vermont.

We're discussing the nature of our relationship and whether or not we think it's been altered by the possibility that we were parent and child in another life.

I say that as far as I'm concerned nothing has changed. If anything, our friendship seems stronger. Maybe what lies at the center of our talk is an unvoiced curiosity about what part Eve plays in our tightly knit karmic scenario, as well as what sort of ties she and I might have had. Are yet to have.

7

Sweet Jane and I are in the Gazebo bookstore, browsing through the books-on-tape section. Jane is looking for something different and challenging to play on the road to New Mexico.

"There's someone I think you should meet," says Sweet Jane. "Her name is Mary Elgin."

"Does she live around here?" I ask.

"Yes. Over near the river."

"The name sounds familiar."

"She's a painter. A very good one. Maybe you've heard of her."

In the week since my past-life regression, Jane and I have spent nearly all of our free time together. It's as if she's become my psychic coach, or guru, and I an avid pupil. Though the nature of our discussions hasn't seemed particularly spiritual or philosophical, I feel as if I've absorbed a great deal of knowledge in a very short time.

"When can I meet her?" I ask.

"Well, how about right now? She just walked in the door."

I turn to see a slender, dark-haired woman entering the shop. She is wearing loose white cotton slacks, a crimson t-shirt, and a mushroom-colored fedora. Sweet Jane waves, and the woman smiles through the aisles, coming toward us. She has shockingly blue eyes and she's fifty maybe, though it's difficult to tell because her face is ageless.

"I was just telling Sunny she needed to meet you, and here you are," laughs Jane.

Mary is alert and attentive, yet somehow distant as introductions are made. As she briefly takes my hand, I feel a surge of power entering me, a current of extremely focused laser-like energy. We make eye contact for a very long time and I feel as if she's appraising me, though not in a physical way. The top of my head begins to tingle.

When Sweet Jane tells Mary she'll be leaving tomorrow, Mary suggests we stop by her house later for a drink.

"Sounds good," says Jane, and I nod in agreement.

We browse at books a while longer and I scan the poetry section, finding nothing new since the last time I was here. When my lunch hour is up, Jane drops me off at Eve's and says she'll be by my house around eight and we'll go see Mary.

"How was lunch?" asks Eve as I enter the house.

"Rushed, I'm afraid. I never got around to eating."

"Go fix yourself a sandwich," she says. "There's stuff in the refrigerator."

"Okay."

"How's Jane?" asks Eve. Since the age regression, her opinion of Sweet Jane has undergone an impressive transformation.

"Fine. She's leaving tomorrow."

"Does she have to? I was hoping she could do one of those hypnosis thingies on me."

"Yeah, that would be nice," I answer from the kitchen. "We can probably find someone else to do it. She wants to leave tomorrow because the people who own the land she's camped on are back from Europe."

"The Nelsons are back? Good. They're some of my better clients."

"Jane thinks their land is haunted. She's glad to be going."

"Haunted? How?"

"Remember the night we were out there and we saw those weird flashing lights back in the trees?"

"Yes."

"Jane thinks it's aliens."

"UFOs?"

"Mmmmm-hmmm."

"Somehow that doesn't surprise me."

Secretly, I'm rather amazed that Eve hasn't dismissed the whole subject as garbage. I join her in the front office with my big sandwich.

"I met somebody today at the bookstore," I tell her. "Really interesting. Her name's Mary Elgin and she's an artist."

"Sounds familiar. Is she a Druid or something?"

"A Druid? I wouldn't know."

"Not a Druid exactly, but isn't she the one who does those ancient Celtic paintings of wizards and magicians?"

"I don't know, Eve. Jane and I are going over there tonight and I'll probably find out."

☾ ☾ ☾

Mary's house is on East Mountain Road, overlooking the river. It's built into the side of a cliff, so the front porch stands on stilts and the rest is made of native limestone and whitewashed planks, with a screened porch running the length of the second-story balcony. This is her studio. It looks to be a very old house, probably turn-of-the-century. Jane tells me that when the city was first founded, the wealthy summer people built the Victorian homes like the one I'm renting, and their servants stayed up in the more modest bungalows and cottages here on East Mountain.

The yard is terraced and filled with coral impatiens and red and green caladiums. A small, hand-painted sign hangs near the door, announcing the Mary Elgin Gallery. There's a white van in the drive, and a pink scooter on the porch. A potbellied pig watches us from inside, peering out behind lace curtains.

"That's Larchmont," giggles Jane.

Mary comes to the door smiling, invites us in. The room is airy and uncluttered, with very simple furniture and lots of wooden things, nature things. There are plants and stones and glassware. Larchmont squeals, hurrying over to greet us. She's a burnished coppery-brown color, about twice the size of a grown cat, and personality-wise she's a cross between a dog and a cat. When I hold out my hand to her she sniffs it warily like a dog, but when I reach down to pet her she rubs against my ankles like a cat. I keep expecting her to purr.

She follows us demurely into the kitchen, which is done in yellows and blues. Mary hands us crystal glasses thin as tissue paper, and points to the refrigerator.

"Help yourself," she says, and goes off to answer the phone.

Jane opens the door. Side by side on the top shelf we see three five-liter containers of wine: white grenache, blush, and zinfandel.

This is my kinda woman.

On a shelf beneath the wine are some hors d'oeuvres. When Jane samples one, Larchmont bursts into mad squeals, demanding her fair share.

Through a side door that exits the kitchen, we follow a path edged in red salvia to some narrow stone steps. It leads us down to a tiny patio carved out of the hillside. A full moon is rising above the treetops and Jane asks if I can see Roy Orbison in it.

"Right," I say. "I think it'd take a little more than wine for me to see Roy Orbison in the moon."

"No, really," she insists. "If you really try you can see his big black glasses, and his soulful eyes, and his nose, and then the rest of his face. And he's singing 'Only The Lonely.' See it?"

I blink, and look, and look again. "Well, yeah, maybe...."

"You really need binoculars to get the full impact," she grins.

Mary joins us, carrying the snack platter, with little Larchmont tapping along behind on the cobblestones.

After several glasses of wine, the insistent singing of tree frogs is strangely hallucinogenic. Larchmont is resting comfortably in my lap. Once again the top of my head begins to tingle. Mary is asking me why I like poetry so much and I say it's like a coded language to me, very primal yet highly refined, very Zen-like sometimes...and then I smile and say I'm often accused of being a misplaced tourist on Earth.

Mary is looking at me intently.

"I want to know you," she says, with conviction. Not I want to get to know you, or I want to know you better, but I want to know you. No one has ever said this to me before, and in so forthright a manner. Flattered but a little confused, I nod, and the tree frogs chorus passionately.

"A tourist on Earth, eh? Mind if we take some brain samples?" smirks Jane.

Another hour or so of talking and it's getting late. Our alfresco session is interrupted by a sudden cloudburst with heavy, insistent raindrops which the tree limbs can no longer deflect. We climb the steps to the house as lightning flares just yards away.

By the time we're settled inside, it's pouring. No use trying to drive home in this deluge, says Mary. Would you like to see my studio?

We troop up a very steep wooden stairway to the second floor and Mary leads us through the bright yellow door to the balcony. She switches on a light and I see that we are in a long, busy room full of easels and canvas and painting supplies.

She explains that having an open-air studio is a good thing because it diffuses the paint fumes, but adds that in damp weather, or winter, it sometimes poses problems. She lifts a plastic tarp to reveal a work in progress.

It's a large piece, in oil, done mainly in blues and greens. By the light of the storm it looks especially compelling. The painting shows a dense, enchanted-looking forest beneath a crescent moon, with the barely discernible shapes of elves and goddesses entwined with the foliage. To the right is a cavernous pool filled with moonlight, and it appears to be bottomless.

The scene is vaguely familiar, though I can't quite recall where or when I've seen it...maybe in my dreams? The overall impact of the painting is haunting.

"I call it 'Dreamlight,'" she says.

Other canvases are propped nearby. Some are only partially completed, others appear ready to be framed, and some appear to have been abandoned. I ask Mary if she ever paints Druids and she replies that yes, after moving here from southern California, Druidic themes were all she painted for several years. The paintings became a well-known, popular trademark and established her reputation. But she seldom does them anymore.

"I didn't want to get locked into a particular style," she explains. "As you can see, I'm experimenting with dreamwork now. Subliminals. And every so often an archetype."

The storm picks up a new intensity and rain falls in glistening sheets from the overhang above the screened windows. Mary replaces the drape on her painting just as a flash of light illuminates the yard and the entire backside of the house.

We exit the studio and Mary shows us the remaining bedrooms upstairs, explaining that this house was once an inn. The rooms are still furnished but are seldom used, and Mary suggests we stay here tonight, considering the streets are probably flooded. Jane and I agree that this is probably a very wise idea.

Since they've been friends for several years and Jane's nomadic lifestyle keeps them apart so much of the time, Jane and Mary stay up very late and talk. I go off to bed in the "green room," lulled to sleep by the sound of rain drumming against the windowpanes.

When I wake again it is daylight, but the rain continues. I yawn and stretch, feeling rested. I get up slowly and descend the stairs. The old house is cool and damp and very quiet.

The kitchen is dark but Mary is just coming out of her bedroom, tying the sash on her robe.

"Good morning," she beams.

The door is ajar and I catch a glimpse of Jane burrowed luxuriously beneath the blankets. No wonder Mary's beaming.

"Like some coffee?" she asks.

"I'd love some," I say, and excuse myself to phone Eve, to let her know I'll be late this morning.

"Don't worry," Eve yawns into the receiver. "Things're gonna be slow today. My power's out. Where are you?"

"Mary's."

There's a very long pause.

"Jane and I got stranded in the storm last night and stayed over."

"Oh. Well then."

"I'll get there when I can," I say.

"All right. Thanks for calling, kiddo."

As I hang up, Sweet Jane glides into the kitchen.

"Helluva storm," I greet her. "I just talked to Eve and her electricity's out."

"Looks like I may not be getting started for New Mexico this morning after all."

A bolt of lightning zigzags past the windows and Larchmont lowers her head and clacks across the linoleum to her velvety bed in the broom closet.

The rain continues all morning. Mary loves storms and is anxious to get to work in her studio. She invites us to stay, but Jane is restless.

The old white Impala fires up faithfully and we angle slowly down wet, winding streets to the center of town, taking about twice as long as normal because trees and power lines are down in places. We stop by my place to get Bennington. She's moping in her dog house, head on her paws, grumpy from no breakfast. I load her in the back of the Impala.

Jane gears way down and we gun our way through axle-deep ponds, the Impala performing nobly like a grand old sled. Sweet Jane's beefy forearms rest lightly on the wheel as she navigates expertly through old boards, tires, beach balls and other floating debris.

At Eve's we find Eve and her seventy-something neighbor Fran swigging coffee in the kitchen. Fran's poodle J.J. greets Bennington with a yap and a wag of his tail, and the two commence their spirited brawling from room to room while Olga, sprawled in Eve's lap, looks on with disdain.

Eve is barefoot and wearing her kimono. Even with bed-hair and deep circles under her eyes, she's gorgeous.

"Oh, Fran, this is the woman I was just telling you about," Eve says excitedly, jumping up. "Fran, this is Sweet Jane, the one who does past-life readings. Fran and I were just talking about the bond we've always felt between us."

"That's right," Fran nods.

"How interesting," says Jane, snagging a chocolate-glazed donut from a large, squashed box on the table.

"Do you think you could do a reading on me?" Eve asks hopefully.

"Sure," says Jane, with a wink. "Some day."

For the rest of the morning, while the Kahlua holds out, Fran regales us with her tales of gold panning, as a youngster in the High Sierras. By early afternoon the skies have cleared, and it's back to work, work, work as usual.

8

It's nearly midnight on Wednesday. I'm stretched out on the old brown sofa at Eve's, and she's sitting next to me on the floor. A candle flickers softly. I've had two rum and cokes, and my body feels heavy. Eve's face is just inches from mine. I repress the urge to trace her cheek, her nose, her lips with my finger.

"You know, I'm very attracted to you," I say quietly. But as soon as the words are out, I want more than anything in the world to crawl beneath the cushions.

Eve turns to me slowly.

"I think you know how I feel about you," she says in a near whisper.

Neither of us says anything for a while. The clock in the living room chimes.

"I've been thinking about...us," she says vaguely.

"Yes," I nod. "Me too."

My heart is pounding.

"Would you like another drink?" Eve asks.

There is a long moment of silence.

"No," I tell her. "I'd better not."

"What are you doing Friday night?" she asks, leaning closer.

I say I have no plans.

"Would you like to have dinner?"

"Yes," I tell her.

"We won't have to get up on Saturday, so maybe we

could talk," she says, resting her hand on mine.

"I'd like that," I say, willing myself to breathe normally.

"Think about it," she says, lightly brushing my cheek with her lips. "Let me know where you'd like to go."

"Think about it?" I chuckle to myself on the way home. For the next couple of days, I won't think about anything else.

☾ ☾ ☾

Friday night. It's late. Eve and I have been to dinner and a show, then stop by Dearborn's for coffee. We run into friends there and we talk. On the way home it starts raining, hard. Red and green lights shine up at us from pools of running water.

I park her car in the drive and we race up onto the porch. Just inside the front door, laughing and out of breath, we kiss.

Again. Very close and very slow, as rain drums down on the roof overhead.

Eve talks about responsibility, wonders if it has occurred to me what a physical relationship with her might involve.

Yes, I have thought about this.

She wonders if this is fair to me.

Given the way that I feel, given the friendship, the companionship, the love—yes, I say, wholeheartedly.

What about her?

I've been in love with you all along, she admits.

And the rain on the pavement sounds just like applause.

☾ ☾ ☾

"I know you," Eve says slowly, looking me deeply in the eyes, stroking my hair. "And I've known you for a long time."

She says this to me after we make love.

"I *know* you," she repeats in a whisper, looking pleased

yet sounding puzzled.

I have felt it, too, this knowing.

The strangest thing will trigger it. This morning, for example, out walking in the rain, I see the tall white steeple of a church with its boards washed clean, and it's as if I'm seeing through time, through the eyes of a stranger, no longer sure of myself, yet remembering, vaguely, a feeling, an emotion, a piece of the puzzle. But what?

And tonight, in my arms, rain tapping the window glass like cat whiskers, Eve asks me if it ever seems—

"Yes," I say.

"—like we've been together before?"

And the look she gives me triggers something so deep that it cannot be forgotten, yet so obscure I can hardly remember, and then, as always, the grain of memory is washed away, lost in a tide of uncertainty and confusion.

☾ ☾ ☾

It seems we've kissed for hours and hours; the sheets are a tangled mess, the candles have burned down low. Eve is breathless, she murmurs something that I ignore.

"It'll be okay," I whisper, running my fingers down and down further till she stops me, clenches my wrist, says "Don't" though I'm past caring about precautions and I tell her so. But she smacks me lightly on the cheek, open-handed, bringing me to my senses, and I realize this is the way it has to be with us, and I shake my head to clear my senses, like a puppy emerging from a pool.

As I reach for the nightstand, Eve's soft lips seek the spot where she hit me. The squeak and snap of a latex glove. Such a simple thing. For my sake.

☾ ☾ ☾

It's early evening and I sit on the hard, cool tiles of my kitchen floor, stroking my snoozing dog.

"Look at those narrow, aristocratic feet," I say. "Most definitely a sign of royalty." I begin tickling her little pink and black toes, which makes her nervous. She shakes her head in annoyance, jingling the tags on her collar.

"You sound just like one of Santa's reindeer when you do that. Were you a reindeer in a former life, honey?"

She flashes me a handsome, wolflike grin, and I start to sing "Bennington The Red-Nosed Border Collie." She half-closes her eyes in ecstasy. It doesn't matter what I sing, as long as she hears her name over and over.

Out in the alley I hear the low, predatory rumble of Diane's Jeep, so I grab my things and head for the door. Diane has agreed to drop me off at Mary Elgin's this evening on her way to play tennis with someone named Marcy.

I hop in the Jeep, grin at Diane. She's fussing nervously with her recently-lightened-about-two-shades blonde hair in the mirror.

Diane looks good. "Do I look okay?"

"Flawless," I assure her.

"Really?"

"Really."

She's been working out for months on a Soloflex she bought used, and the muscles in her neck and forearms stand out like Martina Navratilova's. She has on a sleeveless white pullover and matching shorts and a nice pair of hundred-dollar-plus sneakers. She reeks of a new fragrance. It makes me think of sex, I tell her casually.

"Good," she winks. "I guess I'm ready." She scrutinizes herself one last time, adjusts her Armani sunglasses, and we peel down the alley in a cloud of dust.

Mary's new CD player has just been delivered. We're sitting on her couch listing to Mahler and she pours more wine. Not the cheap stuff she had last time, either. A nice Beaujolais.

Mary asks me about my writing and I recall that Eve has just sold some more of my poems to a little backwater publication called *Northern Light.* She congratulates me, offers words of encouragement, although I feel as if Eve is more the one to be congratulated, she's put forth most of the effort.

I ask Mary what she's been working on and she jumps to her feet and beckons me to follow. We climb the stairs to her balcony studio. Almost dusk, there's just enough light to see without turning on a lamp. She takes my arm and guides me to the middle of the room and we stop in front of a water scene, a huge canvas at least 8 feet by 12 feet, with gleaming, silver-lilac waves in the foreground.

I stand transfixed for several minutes, observing what seems to me an ocean or a pool turned inside out...poor choice of words...churning water, shining droplets—I'm completely absorbed by its mood.

The top of my head is tingling. Mary looks at me attentively and I'm convinced she senses I'm about to say something.

"I remember this," I say. But why?

I seem to recall an alley, at dusk, an alley leading to what was once a carriage house, or an inn, on the waterfront...peeling white paint and a door rather loose on its hinges. A blue lantern hangs by the door. I am with someone. He opens the door and we go inside. A friend long ago used to live here...above the tavern part. A woman gliding down the stairs smiles a dazzling smile. Her gown of blue silk rustles as she reaches out to me, and there is a stirring in my groin....

Whoa. I squeeze shut my eyes, then step back from the painting.

Maybe it's the wine.

It's as if I've just had a flashback of some kind. But to when? And where?

"That's a very powerful painting," I say, feeling quite shaken.

The night creatures are thrashing in the trees. Once again, Mary and I sit outside on her little stone patio at the end of a rocky spiral path off her back door. Larchmont is comatose in my lap. As long as I keep rubbing her fat little belly, she lies still, snoring lightly. After my hallucinogenic reaction to her picture, Mary suggested we come out here for a while. I ask how long she's been a painter.

"About three years."

Is that all?

She nods. The moon hangs above us like a crystal chandelier.

"What did you do when you were living in California?" I ask.

She designed software.

"And you didn't paint until you moved here?"

She shakes her head slowly, emphatically.

"Well then. You just woke up one morning and decided to become an artist?"

"Not exactly. After my heart attack, Sunny, I decided the stress wasn't worth it, and I retired."

Yak, go the tree frogs.

Leaning forward, Mary pours the last of the wine and embarks on a most curious tale.

During the years prior to her heart attack, she says, her life was fairly meaningless, robotic. Spent in mindless pursuit of material goods and security, her days seemed to lack any kind of integrity, conviction, or joy. She worried constantly about losing her job.

She began seeing less and less of her old friends, who probably gossiped about the changes in Mary's behavior and attitudes. She didn't care. She didn't want to be who she was anymore. She wanted to walk away from it all. She started spending her time off alone, wandering in the mountains.

After a particularly stressful week at work, Mary suffered a heart attack and came very close to death. Afterwards, she says, big chunks of information were missing from her life. Nothing seemed quite the same. The thought of returning to the same job she'd had for twenty-eight years seemed ludicrous. The very idea of a two-hour freeway commute each day seemed absurd and hilarious. She wasn't even sure she remembered how to do it.

Contemplating her situation during weeks of cardiopulmonary therapy, Mary realized something was different. Something was wrong. Very wrong. Or, perhaps, something was very right.

Mary quit her job. She sold her house. Tying a scarf over her eyes, she spun herself around, and stuck a pin in a map and the pin landed here, in Renfield. And that, she tells me with a flourish, is how she came to be in our midst.

"So you're telling me that you became somebody else?"

"Yes, I feel that I have. Oh, I know it sounds like a lot of foolishness. But how else do I account for the fact that as soon as I picked up a brush after all of this happened, I was an artist, and a very skilled one at that? Sunny, I've never had an art lesson in my life."

"So you're telling me that when your body died, your old soul exited and this new one, that of an artist, walked in?"

"Yes, Sunny, I believe that's what happened. I'm what they call a 'walk-in.' And you know," she smiles, "I've had a remarkable distaste for computers ever since."

☾ ☾ ☾

"A 'walk-in'?"

Eve's not buying any of this. We discuss it the following morning.

"You wanta know what I think? It sounds to me like

she's got multiple personalities, and they're all named Mary!"

"I don't know, Eve." I relate my account of the painting, how I remembered fragments of a dream when I saw it.

"God, what a crock. The old babe's not content to try and seduce you, she wants to dream with you, too."

"Eve!"

"I don't like any of this. It sounds like mind control. It sounds like..." Eve goes on but I'm not listening. I'm thinking about the way I felt when I stood in front of Mary's painting. It was like suddenly waking into a dream, or being abruptly jolted to another place and time. It reminded me of those compelling sorts of dreams we have that can linger and haunt us all day long. It reminds me, very much, of déjà vu.

☾ ☾ ☾

Saturday.

Diane examines herself in my full-length mirror, flexes her biceps.

"Whatta ya think?" she asks me worriedly.

"Pure brawn," I say with a smile.

"No, really. Can you see a difference? Should I increase my workouts?"

"No, Diane, I think you look just fine. Great. You really do. You're in excellent shape. Don't you think so, Eve?"

"Hot. Totally hot," says Eve, bored, lying on my bed buffing her nails. She doesn't even look up.

Diane's having a new roof put on. The commotion and racket is driving her crazy so she's spent most of the afternoon over here with me. But she's leaving in a few minutes to go have her photo taken, a portrait for the jacket of her new book.

"Does my hair look okay?"

"Cool hair. Yes," I tell her.

I'm not exactly sure why Eve is here. She dropped by

earlier with a fifth of Old Charter and has been lying around moodily ever since. I have just returned to my bedroom following a shower.

"My, my," notes Eve hoarsely. "Don't we smell divine."

"You going somewhere?" Diane asks. She has unbuttoned her pants and checks her abdominal muscles in the mirror.

"Sunny's having dinner with Mary Elgin," Eve chimes.

"Oh yeah? Far out. Who's Mary Elgin?" Diane has rebuttoned her pants and is watching the veins in her neck stand out as she clenches her jaw.

"The artist who painted the picture that's going to grace the cover of your new book," I remind her.

"Oh." She's checking her teeth now, her gums. "Well, tell her I said hi."

"Maybe she'll fix Chinese food. Then you two can have a WOK-in dinner," Eve notes dryly. She's been a grouch all week.

"She can't hear you," giggles Diane. "She's in her WALK-in closet."

"What're you wearing?" Eve asks.

"I don't know. My sage-green pants."

"Don't wear those," she warns.

"Why not?"

"Just don't. They hug your ass."

"So?" I ask, indignant. Then, "Do they really?"

"Something in a nice burlap, perhaps?" Diane offers. "Total body wrap, opaque modesty panels?"

"Shut up," Eve exclaims.

Diane rolls her eyes at me, mouths *What a Bitch.*

"Well, kids," she says, "I do hate to break up this delightful chat, but I really must be going."

"What a relief," mutters Eve.

"Eve darling, you really needn't be so endearing," Diane winks, checks herself one last time, heads out the door.

I slide into my sage-green pants and put on the very expensive white linen blouse Diane bought me on her trip. I start to tuck it in.

"Leave it out." says Eve. "It looks nicer."

I tuck it in.

Eve mutters something under her breath.

"Excuse me? I didn't quite catch that, hon."

"Deranged. I said she's deranged."

"I see. And to whom are we referring?"

She glares at me. "Your friend Mary."

I'm trying to decide between a pair of Gucci loafers or Birkenstocks.

"Just because she says she's a walk-in doesn't make it so."

Or maybe my old Seaport thongs.

"Well, Eve, she *believes* she's a walk-in, so I guess that's all that matters, isn't it."

Nah. Too casual. Go with the loafers.

"Believing doesn't necessarily make it so."

"Get to the point, Eve."

"For example, just because I believed you were a guy wouldn't mean it was so, would it?" she argues.

"What a novel idea," I smile suggestively, running my finger over her fly. "Why don't we try it and find out?"

She brushes me away, gets off the bed.

"You infuriate me sometimes," she says.

"What'd I say, what'd I say?" I protest innocently.

"And now I suppose you want to use my car for your dinner date?"

"Well, yeah. That was sort of the plan. Come on, Eve. Give Mair a chance. You're being paranoid."

"What time will you be home?" she wants to know.

Well, I guess that all depends on whether or not we go berserk and end up fucking each other's lights out, doesn't it? *Lighten up, Eve,* I want to say. *We're not all like Diane.*

"Ten. Eleven at the latest. You know you're more than

welcome to join us."

"No thanks," she sniffs. "I have some shopping to do."

"Okay, fine. I guess I'll see you later then."

And I'm kissing her goodbye and thinking, *I do love you, Eve, I only wish you knew how much.*

9

The house is dark. A sense of peace fills the air. Beside me, Eve mumbles in her sleep. She's on her side, one knee up as if she's climbing sharp stairs in the night. I kiss the top of her head, move her hand from my thigh. Her breasts glow in the moonlight like ripe fruit. Wild rivers run through her veins.

I climb from the bed, replace the sheet over her motionless figure. Olga glares resentfully from her spot at the foot of the bed, still puzzled by my presence, unsure of my worth.

"She's only that way because you're a dog person," Eve explained this afternoon as we were finishing accounts receivable. "My mother was a dog person too," she had added.

I couldn't recall Eve ever talking about her mother before.

"You had a dog when you were growing up?" I asked.

"Oh, sure."

This was followed by a pause so long I assumed she didn't want to discuss it further. Then:

"A little Yorkie named Columbia."

"Columbia?"

"Yes," she grinned. "Columbia had a very ornate wicker bed out in Mother's studio. I guess I never mentioned Mother painted, did I?"

"No."

"Landscapes and seascapes, mostly. Those two watercolors in my office were hers."

Eve went on to tell about a beautiful day in early September when her mother loaded the Volvo with supplies and they went down to the Cape. It was a school day, but too perfect to pass up, said her mother, so Eve got to cut classes. They drove with Columbia on the seat between them. Eve had just turned fourteen that August.

They painted all day. The sand on their feet was toasty—new shoes that fit like water. Eve smiled at the thought of it, but then her voice had become flat and joyless, like the sound of a bell that has traveled many miles over water.

"It was our last day together," Eve said.

The following morning while she was at school, her mother died of an aneurysm.

The unfinished painting of Provincetown Harbor still hangs by Eve's bed.

☾ ☾ ☾

"Maybe you ought to think about getting back into painting again," I suggest to Eve the next morning.

She looks at me curiously, as if I have suggested she take up mud-wrestling or heterosexuality.

"What makes you think I would want to?" she asks.

"No reason. Just a thought."

She continues to look at me strangely while I pour more coffee.

"I was going over to Mary's today," I add. "Maybe you'd like to come along."

"No thanks. Dillard's is having a sale and I want to go buy a new Sony *Walk-in*. Er, Walk-man."

"Very funny."

"And why are you going over there?" she asks.

Oh, to try out Mary's new assortment of sex toys. Maybe smoke some crack. Indulge in a little devil worship. The usual.

"Just to hang out. It's such a creative atmosphere over there. You'd like it, Eve."

She finishes her croissant. "It's strange you should be bringing this up," she says. "I dreamed I was painting last night."

"See?"

Eve looks really weird all of a sudden, like she's on acid or something. I touch her hand but she says it's okay.

"I dreamed about Mother," she says at last. "I was painting a picture of Mother."

Later, we go to Mary's. I don't know why Eve has changed her mind, but we go in her car, and she drives. Mary comes to the door, distracted, brush in hand, a strand of salt-and-pepper hair falling wildly over her forehead. She is wearing faded jeans, blown out at the knees, and a very old t-shirt which she has put on wrong side out and backwards, with the tag sticking up in front.

"Come in, come in," she beams.

"Mary, this is—"

"Eve Phillips," Mary cuts in. "I'd know those eyes anywhere."

I feel as if I've missed an important connection somewhere.

"Your father is Bradley Phillips, isn't he?" Mary asks, smiling broadly.

Eve is smiling too, and their hands are clasped. They gaze at one another like long-lost friends.

"It's so good to meet you, Eve. Your father has told me so much about you."

"Is Dad your physician?"

"Oh yes. And a close personal friend as well. Your father performed bypass surgery on me four years ago."

Small world.

"Is he still living in the Bay area?"

Yes, Eve tells her.

Such a lovely man.

"Oh, but you must forgive my rudeness," Mary rushes on. "I've been up all night working and I've completely lost track of the time. Eve, would you care for a drink? Sunny, will you show Eve around the studio? And while you're doing that I'll get cleaned up and then we can all have a nice lunch somewhere. Doesn't that sound nice?"

Over lunch at Huntoon's Eve and Mary chatter non-stop, mostly about painting.

"Ambiguity is at the core of all art," I hear them saying.

Mary lights Eve's cigarettes. She orders more champagne. She never takes her eyes off Eve, and now it's my turn to be jealous.

Stop hovering, I want to scream.

Hey Eve, how about dazzling us with one of your side-splitting walk-in jokes now? Hey somebody, look at me. How's your entree, Mair? That hedgehog baked in clay to your liking? Those tofu dumplings pretty yummy?

"I want," Mary is crooning, "to know you."

10

Eve's on this new kick. For the past week all she'll eat are Nutri-Grain cereal bars. Raspberry and strawberry. The empty wrappers are everywhere.

Her house is a wreck. I haven't slept in my apartment for days. She wants me to move in with her.

I want to, yes. But it wouldn't be fair to abandon Kim like that. She'll be back in a couple of weeks, in time for school to start. Besides, Eve, your messes would drive me insane. Look at all these fucking wrappers.

She accuses me of being rigid, anal-retentive.

"I'll bet even your junk drawer is tidy, isn't it?" she asks rather loftily.

It is.

Eve looks tired. The long hours have taken their toll, her white blood cell count is way off. Between her father and the trust fund Grandmother Phillips left her, we both know Eve doesn't really need to work at all. Ever.

☾ ☾ ☾

We're lying in bed watching *42nd Street*, one of my favorite movies. Eve leans over and kisses me in such a way that I know we're going to have sex when this is over. But it's late, and I can barely keep my eyes open. All I really want is to lie in her arms feeling her warmth and softness. She's running her hands through my hair, stroking my scalp, caressing my ears. Like a breeze.

A sea breeze. Smell of the ocean. All is calm. If only I could stay like this forever, feel the wind rushing past. I am the lookout. I climb the masthead, scan for whales.

Always, the storm. Black sky, freezing spray that cuts like the dull blade of a knife, crack of the mast as the ship goes down, my lungs fill up with ice.

The choking. Thrashing. Legs and arms won't work. Heavy, heavy. Numb as a bag of stone. A voice calling out to me. Shaking me. Sunny, wake up.

Eve. She's shaking me. "You all right?"

"Yeah, I think so."

"Here." She gives me a sip of her drink, then pulls me close. "Having that dream again?"

Yes. And it's always the same.

"It's only a dream, Sunny, only a silly dream."

But we both know it's something more.

My head on her breast, we sleep.

☾ ☾ ☾

We have just returned from a very late dinner at Holly Kaufman's with her girlfriend Boots, Diane, and Marcy Van Packer. Just as the clock chimes midnight, we walk into the cool, dark hush of Eve's living room, from the soggy grip of August.

As usual, her bedroom and her bed are a wreck.

We lie amidst books, magazines, unopened mail and assorted underclothes. She has pulled off my shirt and undone my shorts. I reach down to open her jeans, slide them off. She rolls over on top of me and presses herself against my thigh. She finishes quietly, in a very short time, still in her panties. I can feel their wetness on my skin. My hands loosen around her waist, and our kiss is very slow.

"Too much foreplay?" I clown, as she collapses beside me. She is silent for several minutes. I listen as her breathing returns to normal.

She leans over, her soft hair falling in my face, her breasts on mine.

"Tell me a story," she whispers.

"What about?"

"Us."

"Okay," I say. "You start."

She considers a moment, then, "On a beach. Sunset. And it's a little bit chilly."

I nod.

"Off season. Cape Cod, maybe. Gulls."

"Yes," I say.

"And dinner's good, you have, um, the prime rib, medium, I think, with herbed potatoes and salad, I have the swordfish with cranberry sauce."

"Say what we're wearing," I tell her.

"Tight white pants, big cashmere sweater, a leather jacket; scruffy jeans and a striped top, a red slicker. Sneakers. You're barefoot."

"What're we doing?"

"Walking by the water."

"How does it smell?"

"It smells...kinda spicy. Kind of...prehistoric."

"Is there a breeze?" I ask.

"Not much. Southerly. Nice. But oh, Sunny, it's starting to rain now, and you know what, I don't think we're on the Cape anymore because nothing looks familiar."

"Okay."

"You take my arm and lead me across the beach to a gray stone house. We're getting pretty wet now. Sand is damp. Walking across the porch, through the door, it's windy now, waves are crashing and this house smells...unused."

"Any furniture?" I ask, tracing the curve of her back.

"Not a lot. A table, some chairs. We're going upstairs. They're creaking. I can hear the rain. We're standing in the bedroom, looking out the window at the sea. Everything...gray. The sky, the water, this house."

"Is there a bed?"

"Yes."

"Lie down. Tell me how it feels." I brush the down of her thighs.

"We're bouncing around on it. Very soft and downy. There's a quilt...looks old, feels good. It's chilly in here. Windows are open. Rain coming in."

I slide in three fingers, nonchalant. She sucks in her breath.

"What year is it?" I ask.

Long pause. "Eighteen seventy-six."

"Whose house are we in?"

"I'm not sure."

"Is anybody watching?"

"I don't think so. We're alone."

"Good. This sounds a lot like 'Goldilocks and the Three Bears' and I wouldn't want to get caught, would you?"

"No," she gasps.

"Feeling pretty good?"

"Yes."

"More?"

No reply.

"Is there music playing, Eve?"

"Uhh."

"What? I didn't quite catch that, hon."

"No. Yes. It's..."

"Hmm?"

"...piano."

"Harder?"

"Nnnnnnnhh."
"More?"
Shakes her head. Eyes closed.
"So tell me, Eve, what color are the walls?"
Pause.
"Eve?"
"They're...yellow."
"I thought you said everything was gray."
"Gray. Don't stop. I mean they're gray."
"Yellow? Gray? Which is it?"
"Wallpaper. Yellow and gray wallpaper. With roses."
"Ahhh. Must be nice. Is the scent of roses overpowering?"
"Mmmmm-hmmmm."
A little faster.
Good, baby.
"Music still playing?"
Nods.
"Who's it by?"
"Clara Schumann."
"Oh, nice choice. Still raining?"
"Yes...it's...pouring."
"Wallpaper still the same?"
Wrapping her legs around me.
"It's a very real place, you know."
Wet sounds.
"Sunny, I love you."
Her fingers in my back.
"Eve, I love you more."
Up and over my shoulders.
"Please don't ever leave me."
High tide, waves crashing on the pier.
"I won't."
Painting ourselves into a picture.
"Smell the roses?"

Arches her back.
"Yes yes yes."
And looks into my eyes.
"Eve."
Remembering, both of us, a room, a day, a house.

11

It has been a reasonably quiet morning. Eve seems a little run-down so I suggest she sleep late and let me take over the office for a while. When Diane calls at a little past ten, I recognize her husky voice immediately.

"Ms. Phillips is in a meeting right now," I say, "Can I take a message?

"You sure can. Guess what, Sunny?"

"What?"

"I got the job! I'm going to be teaching again!"

"Great, Diane. But does that mean I'll have to start calling you Dr. Stafford?"

"O Exalted One will do nicely," she snorts.

Eve saunters in wearing robe and sunglasses, comes up and kisses me, whispers "Please come back to bed."

"It's Diane," I tell her. "She got the job."

Eve grabs the receiver. "Diane, is that you? Huh? You're gonna be what? Well, hey, nice going!" Slyly, she alludes to the fact that Marcy Van Packer's dad just *happens* to be the chair of the English department. This is followed by considerable guffawing.

"Yeah, I just woke up." She yawns for effect. "The little management consultant's been minding the store. Mmm-hmm. Say, why don't you swing on by? We'll celebrate."

Diane and Marcy Van Packer come over. Marcy is pale,

elf-like, and wears thick glasses. Her speech is fragmented and erratic as is she's suffering a disorder of some kind, but I attribute it to her very high I.Q. and the fact that, at age thirty, she has finally taken her very first lover, ever.

☾ ☾ ☾

A couple of nights later, Fran is sitting out on the porch with Eve when I get back from the market. Fran is telling about her wild younger days when she prospected for gold in Alaska.

"Those Northern Lights were something else," she quietly reminisces.

"Find any gold?" I ask.

"Oh, some. Blew it all gambling and chasing women, though. Finally gave it up, went south and worked the crab boats for a while. Cold as the dickens."

In the silence that follows, Eve mentions my recurring dream of being at sea in a winter storm. In a little tuna rig, she says.

Actually, it was a whaling ship in the North Atlantic, I correct her.

"Hmm. Could be a past-life memory," Fran pronounces, ripping into the potato chips I've bought, twisting the top off a Pepsi.

Yeah, probably.

☾ ☾ ☾

Eve's drinking and watching TV, getting more and more melancholy as the evening progresses. When I finally tire of writing and come to bed around midnight, there's an old Bette Davis movie on. I think it's *Petrified Forest.*

"What are you going to do, Sunny," Eve asks me, not looking at me as I lie down beside her, "What are you going to do if I get sick?"

"You're not going to get sick," I tell her.

"Will you still love me?"

"You're not going to get sick, Eve."

"Will you?"

It's true. I tense with every sneeze or sniffle now, aware of each new and tiny shadow; every restless night.

"Of course I will," I tell her. "I'll always love you, no matter what."

☾ ☾ ☾

Eve's been behaving strangely all day. Furtive. Secretive. When Snappy Pat, purveyor of fine gossip, calls in the afternoon, Eve takes the phone in the back office and shuts the door. She seems nervous and preoccupied. Distant.

At quitting time she complains of a headache, says she needs rest. I come to my apartment, a place that's beginning to seem forlorn and alien to me, a place I haven't spent more than three or four hours in for the past couple of weeks.

The apartment is hot and stuffy and desperately needs cleaning. Maybe I should hire someone to come in and tidy up before Kim gets back from California. The barren atmosphere depresses me and there's nothing in the refrigerator but some extremely expired yogurt and a bottle of Japanese beer I don't remember buying.

Bennington's cranky. She makes it clear she prefers the climate-controlled comfort at Eve's and resents being shuffled back over here in this heat.

I decide to shower, but when I turn on the water it comes oozing out rusty and thick like old motor oil. I storm into the kitchen, rip open the refrigerator and slam down the beer in about five swallows. Bennington, nose in the air, sneers disdainfully as I belch.

The phone rings. I let the answering machine pick it up and hear Diane's voice:

"I know you're there, Sunny. Answer your phone."

She'll hound me unmercifully if I don't. "Yes, dear?" I

sigh into the receiver.

"Sunny?"

"She ain't here. She's getting a brain transplant. This is the neurosurgeon assigned to the case."

"How loathsome. Ask the little twerp if she'd care to slip across the alley and dine lavishly avec moi."

"She says thanks but she's not hungry."

"Sunny, get your butt over here."

"No. I'm going to hang up now."

"Sunny—" growing shrill, "—what's the matter?"

"Nothing, Diane. I just don't feel like being sociable."

"Come on over. We can talk."

"I'm having a bad day."

"Come on over and we'll get some videos or something."

"No."

"Yes."

"All right, all right," I sigh.

"Good. I'll order pizza."

Before I cross the alley to Diane's, I try calling Eve to see if she is feeling any better, to ask if she needs anything. But there's no answer.

Marcy is composing a cello elegy on Diane's kitchen table. When the pizza arrives we sit munching in silence. Diane's on the phone. I stare out the window, wishing it would rain.

A couple of hours later I borrow Marcy's Volvo on the pretext of driving to the store for Pepsi. I swing by Eve's. There's a strange van in her drive. I slow down as I cruise by. It's a red and white VW in very nice shape. The digital clock on Marcy's dash reads 11:05. There are no lights on anywhere in Eve's house.

I drive home slowly. When I get to Diane's I realize I have been crying.

Diane's in the kitchen. Asks if I remembered the Pepsi.

"No," I say numbly, "I forgot."

Then where have you been?

Just driving.

Sunny, what is it?

Nothing. Tears are falling. I place Marcy's keys on the table and turn to go.

Catlike, Diane is on her feet, an arm at my waist.

"Hey," she says. "What's wrong?"

"I think Eve may be having an affair," I blurt.

Diane starts as if somebody's just slugged her with a dead mackerel. She stares for several seconds, then slowly, deliberately, shakes her head.

"Never."

"Oh, yes. I think so."

"Sunny, no."

"You'd tell me if you knew anything, wouldn't you?"

When our eyes meet she averts her gaze.

"Just trust me on this," she says, tight-lipped. "Come on, enough of this."

Despite my weak protests, Diane wrestles me into the bedroom where Marcy snores contentedly on the king-size bed. "You're staying with us tonight."

☾ ☾ ☾

I can't wait to start writing in my journal, the dark green spiral notebook Diane handed me through the window of my VW van, my Grateful Dead bus, at the very last minute on my way out of town.

Friday morning, Diane had insisted on taking me to work in her Jeep. When we pulled up to Eve's and I saw the van still parked in her drive, my heart sank. Had Eve overslept? Was I going to stroll in there and find my sweetheart with someone else? My heart pounded so frantically beneath my thin t-shirt I was afraid Diane would see it.

But as I climbed the porch steps there sat Eve in the swing, surrounded by a halo of emerald morning glory vines, smiling her Mona Lisa smile.

"Whose van?" I blurted before we'd kissed or touched or said hello.

So when she tossed me the keys and said Yours, I must've looked as if I was having an out-of-body experience.

Two days later I left Renfield, headed north to the mountains.

Eve had conspired with Snappy Pat to find exactly what I'd wanted in a camper, even down to the color. Pat put in a new motor, clutch, and brakes. Eve kept pressuring her to have it ready in time for me to take a short vacation before school began.

"How are you going to manage without me?" I had protested to Eve at first, hands on hips, reluctant to go. Then, realizing how silly that must sound, I grinned and ran home to pack.

Have you ever had the feeling that certain things happen in life as a way of preparing us for other things? Have you ever had the feeling that unseen hands might be at work during those times when we're so compelled to do something that we go ahead without thinking?

This was one of those times. It was a time when I had to get away, be alone for a while, even though it felt as if Eve and I had become inseparable. I needed this trip. Eve knew it before I knew it, and neither of us knew why.

After finding a beautiful spot to camp I pull out the journal and begin. "I came to the woods," I write, "because I needed time off from my life."

☾☾☾

The first night out, my dog and I camp on the banks of the Shadow River. From the moment I park the van I can feel the energy. Bennington senses it, too. My old roommates Trish and Trish told me about this place. Mystery and legend surround it. Much spirit activity here, it is said. If one is wise, one comes to Shadow River bearing gifts.

"When the moon rides the crest of that lonely hill, she will be there, riding her pony over the ridge and into the trees, her shotgun across the saddle, her jug of corn liquor slung from the saddle horn. Her silhouette is often seen on a rise above Shadow River where she pauses to unhook the jug, lift it in the crook of her elbow and take a long, hard drink. Elvie Hawkins, they say, had a powerful thirst...."

So reads "The Legend of Shadow River" in my *Lesbian Trails* guidebook.

"For nearly a quarter of a century," the story continues, "Hawkins and her marauding band of pioneer women eluded sheriffs and deputies in the foothills of the Pine Forest region."

According to legend, the Shadow River Gang had a considerable amount of gold, and were said to have stashed their loot in a cave deep in the woods. My friend Snappy Pat claimed to have found that cave several summers ago, but once inside, her companion was bitten by a snake, and they were forced to retreat.

As Snappy Pat tells it, she had to drag her feverish, semiconscious partner mile after endless mile through bogs and dense foliage until at last they encountered a somber figure on horseback. Tall, spare, leatherclad, and with a face like granite, she was the quintessential Marlboro woman. Dismounting, the stranger surveyed the injury, then sterilized it with an all-purpose tonic of some sort, after which all three women drank thereof.

"It had the kick of a mule," said Pat.

"Pretty soon it got to raining so hard we couldn't see, and the stranger led us down this little embankment to where there was a cabin hidden in the trees. We went in and stretched out by the fire. My friend fell asleep, and the stranger and I ate some jerky and then finished off the last of her tonic.

"I got so tore down I couldn't uncross my eyes. The last

thing I remember was the stranger admiring my Swiss Army knife. So I gave it to her out of gratitude, and I saw her slip it into a leather pouch with the initials EH ornately tooled on the flap...."

When Snappy Pat woke, the fire was out, the rain had stopped, and the stranger was gone. She and her friend, much better by now, hiked back to where they'd left the truck, and drove into town to the hospital.

But coming back to the woods the next day, said Pat, everything had looked new and changed. It was all different. It was all strange. They never found the cave again, or the cabin. A fog had swept over the mountain and they could not even see the river.

This isn't actually a campground where I've stopped by the Shadow River, just a spot alongside the road, off the beaten path, bound by high white cliffs on one side, and surrounded with trees, mostly birch and aspen, on the other.

The Shadow River is wide and smooth and emerald green in the long light of sunset, and the silence, after the steady snapping putt-putt of my van, is deafening. You can almost hear yourself think, as my father would say.

There appears to be no one else around so I shed my shorts and shirt and slip into the water. The feeling of cool, liquid silk on my hot, dusty skin is electrifying and exhilarating. Bennington watches from shore, appraising the situation, taking her responsibilities very seriously. I wade in water to my waist, then suddenly sense a presence other than ours nearby. When a dark shadow momentarily clouds the water around me, I start, but gazing up, detect nothing out of the ordinary. No clouds overhead, no fleeting bird has passed me by.

Goose bumps rise on my skin. I head for shore. A light, sudden breeze rustles leaves, makes them chatter as I step from the river, and my nipples harden like ripe pink berries in the mouth of a lover.

Someone is watching me, I can feel it. Yet Bennington ambles pup-like after a turtle, giving no sign of alarm. I dress quickly, hurrying to find some blue cornmeal and tobacco in the glove compartment. In a solemn little ritual I express my thanks for a safe trip.

After a quick supper and before it gets dark, I venture into the woods with a gallon of Patty Euphoria's finest wine and a couple of cigars. These are my offerings for the Shadow River Phantom. I leave the brown burlap bag in a hollow at the base of an oak and hurry back to the van.

Night approaches, shadows abound. Funny clicks and pops surround me, and odd flashes of brightness, like blue lightning bugs, flare between the trees. Far off and muffled, as if from underground, a bell tolls mournfully.

Bennington has not strayed far. Eyes narrowed, ears back, jittery, she tiptoes through the fading light. I notice she's lost her scarf, a tasteful mustard and burgundy plaid, a gift from Olga, yet neither of us express the slightest inclination to go look for it. Maybe in the morning, I tell her telepathically. She glances up and nods.

Back at camp, we lock ourselves securely in the van as a full moon sweeps across the treetops. I arrange my sleeping bag neatly on the bunk in back and curl up beside Bennington. I listen to an owl hooting in the branches outside, and think of Eve's soft lips caressing my body.

☾ ☾ ☾

I sleep without dreams and wake at dawn. Golden light spills through the windows. I make my way to the water's edge, feasting on fat wild berries as I go, mouthful after mouthful till my lips and hands are blue, and into the water I plunge.

The current is swift. On the cliffs above me a flock of white birds explode in a whoosh of wings, like a handful of confetti.

Leaves twitch and turn in the breeze, showing first a

green side, then silver-gray. A melodic bird—what kind I don't know—offers its clear, uplifting flutelike song. I plunge my head under water and come up gasping, sputtering gleaming bits of sunshine on the surface all around me. Upstream I catch sight of a fawn, bending, delicately sipping.

Once again I have the peculiar sensation of being watched. Then, as the surface once again assumes its smooth, mirrorlike finish, I falter. Reflected just above my shoulder I see three riders on horseback, observing me from shore. Ice in my veins, I whirl.

But no one is there.

"Bennington!" I yell, so loud it interrupts the mad piper's overture. My dog is nowhere in sight. I turn back to the river. There, three figures behind me are clearly reflected on the water....

"Bennington!"

She answers from far in the woods, a series of frenzied staccato yelps which I know to be the call of a good rabbit chase.

The gentle light of morning momentarily dims and the air thickens, as if during an eclipse. From the riverbank, voices, and the sound of hoofbeats receding into the timber. But my eyes detect nothing.

My fear turns to anger as I clamber ashore.

"Hey!" I yell, resenting this strange intrusion. I scamper barefoot over the rocky ground.

"Hey you!" I shout, annoyed at the thought of intruders lurking nearby.

Following the faint sound of their hoofbeats through the trees, darkness closes around me like a velvet glove. I nearly collide with an enormous spider web blocking my path, easily five feet across and shimmering with dew.

There comes a rustling through the trees and Bennington joins me, wild-eyed, muddy, burrs in her coat. She yips a wild greeting and I hug her neck, suddenly feeling rather silly and vulnerable out here all alone. She licks me affectionately and as we turn to go, a sudden flash of red through the trees catches my eye.

A scrap of cloth, resting at the base of a tree.

Drawing closer, I become aware of a familiarity with this particular tree. It looks a lot different in daylight, but it's the same tree where I left the goodie-bag last night.

Bennington sprints ahead, sniffs at the trunk, quickly looks up at me. There, folded neatly, lies her missing scarf.

The goodie-bag is gone.

Far off in the distance, the wind carries voices, and the sound of women's laughter floats musically through the air.

☾ ☾ ☾

Inside the green spiral-bound notebook journal she gave me, Diane had thoughtfully included a recent snapshot. In it, Eve stands with her arms around me, smiling. We're in the kitchen at Diane's. Both of us look like we've just been shot from cannons. Eve's wearing her robe. My eyes are crossed and my hair looks like an explosion. There's a radiance surrounding us that extends out in all directions.

What surprises me is how fragile Eve looks, her skin like the glaze on fine porcelain, the veins in her wrists and hands showing blue. I glance at the picture, which is now taped to my dashboard, and my heart lights up.

My little camper purrs faithfully along the winding mountain roads. I whiz past a signpost for a nearby church.

"Though I be absent in body," it reads, "yet am I with you in spirit."

☾ ☾ ☾

Late afternoon. Bennington and I have tramped deep in the woods and stop to rest by a waterfall. I have seen no beer cans, Juicy Fruit wrappers, cigarette butts, Swiss Miss pudding containers, empty potato chip sacks, dirty Pampers or discarded condoms for well over two hours now. I have seen, however, several deer, a bobcat, two hummingbirds and a mountain bluebird. I climb up on a huge granite boulder and imagine myself in South America charting the Amazon. I'm thinking about something Diane said one time when I remarked that everyday life with its routines, drudgery and mediocrity can be so draining. If I could just run away and live in the woods, I had said, I'd probably be more inclined to write every day, as you do.

"Ordinary sentences are what make a writer," she said. "Just write, Sunny. Save the magic for later."

☾ ☾ ☾

Winstead's Grocery is a run-down country market on an old logging road deep in the mountains where I've stopped for gas. Bennington swaggers over and strikes up a friendly conversation with the redbone hound that lounges on the porch.

I pass through the creaky screen door and stand in line on the plank floor in front of the cash register, waiting to pay for my gas and a jumbo bag of peanuts. An old Elton John song is on the radio.

The next thing I know, tears are sliding down my cheeks.

"Blue eyes," he croons, "Baby's got blue eyes...."

I step out of line and pretend to browse at postcards. All of a sudden I have the overwhelming urge to talk to Eve, to hear her voice, though we've only been apart for two days. I miss her terribly, and the song evokes such a powerful image that I'm utterly compelled to call her. I hurry outside to a pay phone and call collect. It rings and rings. No answer.

Oh well, I decide, drying my eyes. I'll try again a little later.

☾ ☾ ☾

The hitchhiker I've picked up tells me her name is Maggie Two Trees. I see her walking along the side of the road with bags of groceries, and when I stop to ask if she would like a ride, she peers calmly in the back of my van.

"Your dog bite?" she asks in a flat monotone.

"No, but if you've got any sliced ham in there, watch out. She's quick and sly."

Maggie grins and climbs in gracefully, thanking me for stopping. As I ease the van from the gravel shoulder onto the blacktop, she tells me that her own truck has been dysfunctional for quite some time now. But it's really not that far from the market to where she lives, in Valley of the Clouds.

"Cloud Valley?" I ask, remembering a ski resort by that name nearby.

"No," she says patiently. "Valley of the Clouds."

"Oh, I see," I say, puzzled, not seeing at all.

"When developers came in they changed the name," she explains. "Got it backwards."

Maggie tells me she has lived in these mountains all her life, as have her parents, her grandparents, her great-grandparents. When greedy Anglos came searching for gold over a century ago, her people were driven from their home, eventually resettling in this valley.

"Turn here," she says suddenly. "It's a shortcut."

I lurch to a halt, nearly upsetting the van, and we swerve off the main road onto a narrow dirt one. Mountain bluebirds dart between the evergreens all around us. The scent of wood smoke fills the air.

As we snake our way through the woods, Maggie tells me she makes pottery and is a part-time singer in a rock-and-roll band. Her partner, Karen, is owner of Snowy Peak Lodge. In season, Karen gives ski lessons to jet-setters at the lodge. Off-season, things pretty much come to a standstill in Valley of the Clouds.

It looks as if I've arrived at the very peak of off-season, I observe, as we roll to a stop in front of the cabin, dodging a snoozing dog, a broken-down washer, an old mattress, and a dented, rusted-out truck on blocks.

"Needs a little work," says Maggie, motioning towards the once-green Dodge. The hood and doors are gone, as is the engine, making it the ideal hideout for swarms of homeless cats.

We're in a clearing nestled high in the side of Mount Dorris. About two hundred yards down the steep, unpaved road to our right is Snowy Peak Lodge, surrounded by several other chalet-style homes and cottages, with a few condos nearby.

Maggie invites me into her cabin. It is built of notched pine logs painted slate blue, with red and white geraniums blooming profusely in window boxes above the rough plank porch.

The afternoon air up here on the mountain is thin and cool. I grab my hooded sweatshirt and help Maggie with her groceries. On the porch of the cabin a muscular blonde woman snores peacefully in a hammock.

"That's Princess," says Maggie, booting open the door.

The smell of fresh bread and chili fills my head. As we're putting the bags on the long wooden table, a yellow and white Ford Bronco rumbles into the yard and several women pile out, stomping noisily onto the porch. One of them rouses Princess with a lusty whoop.

"Honey, I'm home," booms a bright-eyed woman with her leg in a cast. "Oh, hi," she greets me at the door. "Sorry, thought you were Maggie." She smiles at me warmly. "I'm Karen."

"Sunny picked me up down by the sawmill," Maggie tells her partner. "I've invited her for supper. She's here from Renfield."

"Renfield? Really? An old friend of mine lives there," says Karen. "Runs a carry-out. Maybe you've heard of her? Patty Euphoria?"

"Heard of her?" I laugh. "This is too much! Just a

second, I want to give you something."

I dash outside to where my van is parked and hop inside, rummaging for something. A moment or two later I'm back in the cabin, proudly placing a gallon of Patty's famous Bluebird wine in Karen's outstretched hands.

"Small world," we laugh in unison, as her friends gather round.

An hour later there are eight of us reclining on the porch, telling stories. It hasn't taken long for the wine to disappear. Karen, I learn, is a graduate of Renfield. She became acquainted with Patty Euphoria when her varsity rugby team would stop by the Chicken Shack after their games.

Karen's real love is downhill racing. She's been skiing competitively for about ten years. She had hopes of qualifying for the U.S. Olympic team until her freak snowboarding mishap back in March.

She props her broken leg up on the porch railing and winks.

"I'm just an old ski bum lately. I lounge around and let Maggie look after me."

"Don't believe her," says Maggie. Karen works out most of the morning, and manages the lodge the rest of the time.

"Speaking of lodge," says Princess, "what do you say we head down there and eat? I'm starving."

We all pile into the Bronco for a rollicking ride down the hill to Snowy Peak Lodge. The place isn't exactly a beehive of activity. As we traipse through the back door leading into the kitchen, Karen introduces me to the chef, La June, a burly, wisecracking woman with brick-red hair, a former sumo wrestler from Maui.

Dinner's delicious. Free-range chicken with herbed rice and jalapeño cornbread. I sit beside Princess. Maggie and Karen sit across from us. The others, C.J., Babe, M.J. and Tina, are locals. C.J. and Babe have a horse ranch at the foot of Mount Skidmore.

I'm enjoying this bit of local color with slow-talking, levelheaded M.J. She smokes cigars and blows smoke rings, leaning back in her chair with her pants undone to accommodate a very full tummy.

I'm also enjoying the nearness of Princess, whose animal magnetism radiates like a furnace. We are seated next to a mammoth stone fireplace, and I'm unsure which is toastier, Princess and her steady, imploring gaze, or the heat from those smoldering logs. She has shed her little jacket to reveal a black leather vest underneath, nothing else, and the way her curly blond hair brushes against her bare shoulders, and the way the firelight dances on the downy gold of her forearms is just too enticing.

She reaches over, pours the rest of my beer into my glass, smiles. Dessert has arrived and Princess feeds me big forkfuls of her mousse or torte or whatever it is. Karen asks if I enjoyed my meal.

"Absolutely," I say, between gooey mouthfuls of chocolate and pecans.

"Say something poetic," urges Princess. "Don't poets always do that?"

It takes me by surprise.

"*La cigale ayant chanté,*" I smile, "*tout l'été.*"

"Oh yes, yes," she grins, rolling her eyes. "Now translate."

Very slowly, I lean close and whisper, trying to maintain the utmost composure.

"The grasshopper sang all summer."

Just down the hill from Snowy Peak Lodge is the infamous Gold Nugget Saloon, owned and operated by M.J. and her lover Tina. Before it was the Gold Nugget, M.J. carefully explains, it was called Cinderella's, and before that it was the Town Pump. There are still bullet holes in the woodwork dating back to gold rush days. Back when Valley of the Clouds was a rip-roaring mining town, the bar doubled as a bordello under the legendary proprietorship of T.

Esther Hearn.

"T. Esther was my great-great-aunt," M.J. says proudly. Her portrait still hangs in a heavy gilt frame above the polished mahogany bar. When T. Esther died of gunshot wounds at a Mardi Gras parade gone berserk, the Town Pump fell into the hands of M.J.'s distant cousin, an alcoholic drag queen. When he turned the bar into a showcase for drag exhibitions, business went through the roof. The tourists couldn't get enough.

M.J.'s cousin made a fortune. Before packing off to Key West to retire, he turned the place over to M.J., who was mayor at the time.

"I ran them queens outta there first thing," she says. "Didn't care much for the tourists either, but what can you do? I wanted to make this bar into a down-home, easygoing place where you could get some good chili or breaded catfish for lunch. Couldn't think of a fancy name so we just called it the Gold Nugget and it stuck. Caught on really big with the locals."

After our dinner, we set off leisurely in the general direction of the Gold Nugget Saloon. The streets are deserted and I browse in shop windows admiring everything from storybook postcards to Rolex watches.

Cassiopeia hangs like white diamonds in the night sky above us. Princess and I stroll along, with C.J. and Babe behind us. Princess looks over at me and winks. Following along are M.J. and Tina, and bringing up the rear are Karen and Maggie, smiling, arms at each other's waist. Karen moves well for someone with her leg in a cast.

In the soft golden wash of the street lights I feel a sense of peace and magic, as if I've suddenly fallen into a Mary Elgin painting. Princess links her pinkie finger around mine, oh so casually.

The exterior of the Gold Nugget Saloon looks like something out of *Gunsmoke*. There's a weathered boardwalk, a hitching post, a couple of wooden whiskey barrels full of petunias sitting out front, and two large twelve-paned windows on either side of the swinging saloon doors. Princess shoulders her way inside and the rest of us follow.

A grizzled cowboy looks up and nods as we enter, then goes back to his beer. A crew-cut woman behind the bar greets us with a Liberace smile. Balls click seductively over at the pool tables and Dolly Parton wails on the jukebox.

As we amble towards a booth in back I notice each table is decorated with a red and white checkered tablecloth and a candle in a wine bottle. None of that hokey, neon, mid-century-modern crap for M.J. This is a classy little tavern. The seats are leather, not vinyl, and of the many photographs on the walls, I recognize Lily Tomlin, Whoopi Goldberg, and Barbra Streisand, all posing with M.J.

M.J. sips grapefruit juice on the rocks while the rest of us warm up with tequila. Patsy Cline comes on and somebody turns up the volume. Things start to get fuzzy.

I get up to go to the restroom and as I'm splashing cold water on my face the orange-haired crew-cut bartender flounces in. She reminds me of Annie Lennox on steroids.

"Hi hon. Still driving that pink Cadillac?" she asks on her way into the stall.

"Uh..." I say.

"You gonna come by later?"

"Uh..."

"Coco?" she asks. "Aren't you Coco from Orlando?"

Life in a resort town must get hectic at times, I think, as I duck out the door.

12

Maggie has talked me into staying overnight.

"I need you tomorrow," she says. When I try to question her, she places her finger on my lips.

"Later."

Nestled snugly in a feather bed and wrapped securely in a down comforter, I wake groggily the next morning as Bennington nudges me politely with her nose. Standing with her hind feet on the floor and her front paws on the pillow next to my head, she gives an excited little yip of greeting.

Feeling very much like a bedraggled harlequin after last night's carousing at the bar, I yawn, stretch, and crawl gingerly out from beneath the covers, lured by the wonderful aroma of coffee. I can hear Maggie and Karen's soft voices down in the kitchen. Bennington and I tiptoe from the loft and join them.

Several stacks of buckwheat pancakes later, I'm feeling better. Maggie pours me a third cup of coffee, thick as fudge. It is a clear and beautiful morning. Karen is outside hanging wash on the line. Bright blue and red and purple shirts flap in the breeze. Bennington sits at my feet, somewhat mistrustful in this house full of cats.

Maggie wants to know if I'm about ready. She's got the Bronco all gassed up for the mysterious task I'm to help her with this morning. She won't say what it is, only that we need to get going. It's already past ten.

"Here, put this on," she says, handing over her jeans jacket. "You might need it." It has a red flannel lining and a lapel button that says 'How Dare You Assume I'm One Of The Idle Rich!' Somehow, during last night's revelries I seem to have misplaced my hooded sweatshirt.

Maggie takes the back roads, winding mile after mile through dense pine forest in the crisp morning air.

"Feeling better?" she asks.

"Oh, yes," I reply, reveling in the clean, heady aroma of her jacket. "So where are you taking me, Maggie?"

"You'll see." Her smile is inscrutable. Down the mountain we glide, passing log homes and a pond frozen at its edges.

After twenty minutes or so we arrive at a place on the banks of the Powder River. Maggie parks the Bronco next to a grove of aspens. She reaches into her backpack and pulls out a knife in a leather sheath, with at least an eight-inch blade.

"Come on," she says.

She leads me noiselessly down a path along the riverbank, pausing occasionally and sniffing, listening to the wind. The only sounds I hear are quarreling birds and the peaceful whoosh of the river. When we've hiked maybe half a mile upstream through dense foliage, we stop.

I inhale deeply, filling my lungs with the wonderful woody-piney smell. I gaze at the timeless woods before me. Why, this could be another century, I say to Maggie.

She nods, and we stand in silence for several minutes, watching sunlight dance on the water. Then, with her back to me, Maggie reaches up, and using her razor-sharp knife, swiftly begins slicing small branches from a willow. She places each slender stalk in my hands until we have half a dozen.

"There now," she says.

"What are we doing, Maggie?" I ask, still a little drunk, hung over, impatient.

Smiling serenely, her jet-black hair tucked up inside a

Stetson, she stands in a shimmering wedge of sunlight, motionless, at peace with her world, staring across the river.

"You'll see," she says.

Our next stop turns out to be at Thunderwings—C.J. and Babe's horse ranch at the base of Mount Skidmore. Maggie heads for the corral and greets two Appaloosas, Spike and Crunch, by name. She bridles them and leads them from the corral, handing me Spike's reins.

Bareback, we ride away from the house along a path leading through a meadow, then into the foothills. Despite her name, Spike seems well-mannered and gentle. Her coat is a spectacular burnished copper and white. Crunch is a much darker color, nearly chocolate, and she's several hands taller.

As we head up a rocky trail surrounded by white birch and trembling aspen, Maggie reaches over and offers me her canteen. Now that the morning mist has evaporated and the sun has gained momentum, the chill is gone. The air feels dry and warm, almost scratchy. I swallow some of the delicious spring water and slip out of my jacket, engulfed as I do so by its sharp, citrus fragrance.

Maggie hums softly to herself. Though I really want to share my recent experience involving the mysterious Shadow River Phantom with her, and to ask her what it was like growing up in Valley of the Clouds before it became a resort town, the timing doesn't seem right somehow, the mood too fragile. Ever since I stopped and picked her up yesterday I've felt a peculiar sense of expectation, almost as if she'd been waiting for me to come along.

"Maggie," I ask, "what are you going to do with those willow branches?"

She turns and smiles, and we pause at a creek, letting the horses drink. Maggie unscrews the cap from her canteen, drinks deeply, presses the sleeve of her black and red wool Pendleton to her lips.

"We're gonna make some dreamcatchers," she answers, then grins at my blank expression.

☾☾☾

Dreamcatchers, Maggie explains, are used by Native American mothers on cradleboards. Good dreams, she says, pass through the hole in the center and slide down the feather into your sleep. Bad dreams are caught in the web and kept away. But you don't have to be Native American to hang one over your bed for pleasant dreams, she smiles.

Back in the kitchen at C.J. and Babe's, Maggie shows me how to bend the slender stalk in order to make a hoop, just so, which she then decorates with artifacts from our horseback ride: feathers, beads, pine cones, tiny fossils. In summer the branches really ought to be used within forty-eight hours or they lose flexibility, she explains. Using a paint brush and red, yellow, and turquoise paint, she draws symbols and patterns on the hoop as I watch.

C.J. and Babe are gone. We had a very pleasant lunch with them an hour ago. They've driven to the lumberyard on the other side of the mountain and probably won't be back till dark.

Maggie puts finishing touches on the hoop, secures a leather tassel at the bottom, sets it aside. Taking a second stalk and bending it, she says,

"That one is yours, Sunny, and this one will be for Eve."

Maggie begins describing a dream she had of me several nights ago. I was in a mansion full of many doors, on a mission but hopelessly lost, she says, trying to find my way, on a vision quest. When Maggie woke and told her dream to Karen, it had turned out that Karen had been having exactly the same dream: a lonely, red-haired girl, frightened and confused, searching frantically for the right door, trying one after another, calling loudly for her friend.

They had known I was coming, Maggie says. They were expecting me. They knew me by my hair.

"You're one of us," Maggie says, fixing me with her level gaze. "You're a dreamer, aren't you?"

"Yes," I admit, a little surprised and taken aback. "I do some of my most important work while I'm sleeping. But what about my friend?" I ask, referring back to the strange dream. "Do I ever find her? Was it Eve?'

There is a long pause. Maggie is involved tying an intricate knot in a piece of twine hanging from the willow hoop.

"Yes," she finally answers.

"Well? What happens?"

"You find the door. You open it."

"Good," I say.

"But first," she says, holding up the hoop of the dreamcatcher she is crafting, "First you must have this." Her look is solemn. "It will lead you through that door."

"Oh," I reply, thinking that I see. "Like two pieces of a puzzle or something, two halves of a whole...that kind of thing?"

She does not look at me. "Once you find that door, then you and Eve will be together always."

The afternoon shadows have grown long. Between us on the kitchen table at Thunderwing Ranch lie a half-dozen ornate and brightly decorated dreamcatchers. With a flourish, Maggie demonstrates one more time how to waft the hoop through the air, last thing at night before sleeping, to catch oneself a dream.

Outside the weathered old ranch-house we load our things into the Bronco in preparation for the long haul back to Maggie and Karen's. Maggie pops the Bronco in gear and we barrel down the rutted lane to the road that takes us home.

The setting sun illuminates the craggy peaks of nearby Mount Shavano.

"Do you see that patch of white up there?" Maggie asks, pointing.

"Yes," I reply, squinting.

Each spring, says Maggie, when the ice and snow are supposed to have gone, a patch of white always remains near the top of the mountain. It is in the shape of an angel, with arms stretched wide in a benevolent pose. She tells me how early on during the gold rush, her ancestors were driven from their birthplace, and after much hardship, eventually settled here. According to legend, the Angel of Shavano watches over Native Americans so that they will always be safe in this valley.

When we reach the cabin an hour later, twilight is upon us. Bennington dances sideways around the Bronco, barking uproariously as we pull into the yard. Karen greets us at the door, and the enticing aroma of fresh bread and steaming soup reach out a warm welcome.

☾ ☾ ☾

Early the next morning I leave Maggie and Karen's cozy log cabin. A mist hangs over the valley below as I load my van and start it up. Bennington sits perched in the passenger seat, alert and ready for the road again.

Maggie and Karen stand with shoulders touching in the frosty morning light of the yard, looking sleepy, very much in love. Maggie reaches through the window of my van, gives my hand a good squeeze.

"Use that dreamcatcher," she says with a wink.

Earlier she had given me a set of bluish-gray and seafoam-green clay mugs and a teapot, with flecks of lavender throughout. Maggie is a very fine potter. The cups shimmer like peacock feathers in the sun. "For you and Eve," she said quietly, looking away.

I am deeply touched.

"Take care of that leg," I say to Karen. She is scheduled for her fourth in a long series of operations next week. "I expect to see you on 'Wide World of Sports,' this season."

"Right," she says, flashing her million-dollar endorsement smile. On tiptoe, on her good leg, she reaches up to kiss my cheek. "Have a safe trip."

"You'll be back," says Maggie.

"See you next time, then," I nod, adjusting my cap, checking the mirrors. This is hard. I feel such a bond.

Bennington barks farewell as we lurch slowly out the yard, past the old Dodge, past the woodpile and the raggedy, chewed-up mattress. Passing Snowy Peak Lodge, I pause just long enough to shout goodbye to Princess, who's up on the roof installing solar panels. She looks so cute in those big overalls and utility belt. Her boombox blasting, she waves and clowns, blowing me a kiss, and I turn down a woodsy, fragrant road that takes me well beyond the long yellow wall of summer.

☾ ☾ ☾

My dog, Bennington, doesn't really mind being a writer's pet. Oh, my moods and temperament get on her nerves from time to time, she confides. And sometimes she tires of hearing poems read out loud, time and time again, revision after endless revision. But she'll gladly sacrifice that in return for times like this, out here in the wilds under a full moon beside a crackling fire, with a nice dog biscuit and a full tummy, just the two of us, with stars up above shining so big and bright it's almost scary.

All day, we have driven away from the mountains where Valley of the Clouds is nestled, gone through a canyon, gone through some tunnels, wound our way through a pass of breathtaking beauty, and then found another mountain range, finally stopping for the night deep in the woods next to a dry creek bed.

At bedtime we climb dreamily into the van. Eve's picture, taped to the dash, smiles up at me. Touching a finger to my lips I touch her lips in the photo, and nestle down securely in my soft little bed. Beside me on the wall hangs the dreamcatcher, its beads and feathers glowing blue in the moonlight.

Taking the willow branch in my hands, I feel a rush up my spine, a sizzle in my brain. Far down the mountain I hear the yowl of a cat; miles away, the step of a deer.

As I sweep my dreamcatcher through the air above my bed, the low, rolling sound of Maggie's words fills my head:

"Good medicine. Use it wisely."

The air is frigid, the water burns like ice as it slices my flesh. I can hear the wind whistling through North Light's rigging. She buckles and heaves, shrieking as she goes down, and I am out of my body, gliding above black water, freed from the storm.

I rise like mist, drawn towards dawn at the edge of the land, the lighthouse, the sea cliffs, the rocky shore—and I am home.

The elegant old house stands silent and dark on the water-front. I ascend the stairs as if in a dream, bathed in colored light.

I hover at the foot of their bed.

Naked and disorderly in sleep they lie, their arms flung this way and that, the bed sheets wrinkled and matted like crepe paper. I bend and kiss them, my father first, his broad chest heaving like a sail in the wind, his fine, distinguished brow salty and cool beneath my lips.

Whispering words of love, I touch my lips to my stepmother's. She stirs, murmurs in her sleep, gently squeezes my hand.

Down the hallway a child rests in her tiny bed, moonlit curls spilling across an embroidered pillow. Taking her in my arms, I love her till the ache in my heart becomes so much that I turn away.

At the doorway I pause, looking back one last time. Her light fills the room, she glows from within.

Then, like a waking angel, I rise, seeing the silver cords that bind us, all of us, always.

13

I've just driven twenty miles through rain and early-morning fog on treacherous roads to get to a phone because I'm so excited about the dream. I try calling Eve's but I get no answer. Disappointed, I drive aimlessly for a while. The rain has let up and a rainbow arches through the mauve clouds up ahead. When I pass an ancient wooden sign for a place called Vanishing Bridge, I head down the winding road in that direction, feeling almost as if I'm being guided somehow. An hour later, I am lost. Maybe I've entered a time warp? Vanishing Bridge is not on my map, yet I distinctly recall that the sign said it was only six miles. I've been driving along for much longer than that.

"Vanishing Bridge has vanished," I tell Bennington, who sits earnestly in the passenger seat staring straight ahead.

I drive and drive but it only gets us deeper into the mountains. Finally, my stomach growling, I decide it's time for breakfast. I pull off onto a rutted lane that leads through the pines to an open meadow.

The silence is spectacular. There's no noise, not even a bird. The air is still. We're parked in a clearing overlooking a river valley. Bennington jumps down to patrol the area. Mist and fog hang in eerie sheets, and the clouds are low.

I perch among wildflowers in my little lawn chair. Eating my nuts and berries, I feel as if I'm being watched. Bennington noses around over by what looks like a burned-out tree stump on the edge of the clearing.

This peculiar silence reminds me of a story I once heard from an eccentric gunsmith at Silver Dollar City. He told of a mysterious hollow deep in the woods outside Branson where sometimes children could be heard singing. Folks swore they saw flashes of color from out the corner of their eyes: a blonde, fuzzy-haired girl in a flowered feedsack dress peeking out from behind a tree, or rowdy little boys in worn overalls playing leapfrog. Then you'd blink, and they'd be gone.

But the sound of their banter was hollow and raw, and it seemed no amount of sun or blue sky could ever erase the pall that hung over that meadow, that place where no bird sang, no deer set foot. A trapper had discovered their bodies, twelve of them, out behind the old log schoolhouse, their throats cut. Strangely, the body of the schoolteacher was never found.

Indians, they said.

Recalling this century-old story makes me shiver, and I get up to retrieve my sweatshirt from the back of the van. Coming back out, I'm startled to see a white-haired woman slowly making her way through the brush. I'm surprised Bennington's not barking.

As the woman comes closer, I see that she is smiling, and on her arm she carries a basket of what look like wild berries. Her long hair hangs to her waist.

"Hello, Missy," she calls out.

"Morning," I reply.

Her skin is parched as the bark of an old tree, and she surveys me with a sort of grave but amused tolerance. She wears lace-up moccasins over buckskin trousers, and a threadbare denim shirt. She smells of wood smoke. For some reason I'm reminded of Phoenix Jackson, the character from Eudora Welty's *A Worn Path*.

"Lost?" she asks.

"Sort of," I concede. "I came looking for Vanishing Bridge but never found it."

"Looking for what?"

"The settlement. Vanishing Bridge."

"Never heard of it."

"There was a sign back down the road a ways and I uh...I uh...."

"You by yourself?"

"My dog," I say, pointing.

The old woman nods. "She's found the spot."

Her eyes meet mine, and they shine like fire. "Smart hound you got."

"Thanks. Care for some water?" I ask, wondering if she might be deranged.

"Yes, I would. Very kind of you." With both hands, she takes the blue and white enamel cup I am offering, drinks deeply.

A sudden zephyr sweeps the clearing, whisking the tops of nearby trees.

"Come here, young lady," she says. "I'd like you to see something." She beckons, and I follow wordlessly to the edge of the clearing, to the place where my dog sits at the foot of a gnarled stump.

Eve sometimes remarks how unobservant I am. To hear her tell it, I'm in a trance about half the time. There could be a fleet of UFOs overhead, she says, and I probably wouldn't notice. And maybe she's right, because it's several seconds before I discern that what I'm looking at is not a tree stump at all but a very intricate sculpture of some sort.

There are hands and feet and hair. There are lips touching and cheeks caressing and eyes turned heavenward. There is breast on breast and legs entwined. Fingertips kiss the soft down of a belly. Two women, their backs arched, poised, as if for flight.

I stare stupidly at the dark, satiny wood for several minutes. This is no ordinary tourist attraction, I realize. One thing's certain—this wasn't hacked out with a chainsaw. The characters are exquisitely detailed and just too complete...as if...almost as if...and yet, looked at another way, this is just a tree stump. The figures seem to be camouflaged so gracefully within the wood that you can be looking right at it and not see.

"What *is* this?" I whisper.

"You have blundered well," she says to me. "You have found the Loving Tree."

I circle the stump slowly, touching it, admiring it, astonished. Bennington sits on her haunches, grinning, pleased that I have come out of my stupor long enough to appreciate this rare treasure. She basks in the radiance of it.

"Who made this?" I ask the stranger. "Did you?"

"Oh, no child," she says.

Though not tall, maybe four feet at most, the stump is wide at the base. It might have been a huge old walnut tree once, or an oak. What remains has been charred and blackened, and the sides look as if they might be petrified.

"But who are they? How did they get this way?"

The woman just nods and smiles a cagey smile.

"Can the wind feel itself as it blows through the pines?" she asks. "Does a song hear itself being played?"

Lightning, maybe. Yeah, lightning probably struck this tree a long time ago and burned it down and left this really weird, like transmogrification or something—this edifice of two lithe goddesses in a most inspiring embrace....

As luck would have it, there's no film in my camera. But I sense that to try and get a photograph would be not only crass, but impossible.

"Many have sought in vain," says the old woman, her voice trailing off. She smiles at me with rich brown seal-eyes, and her hair is a sea of cotton in the pale morning light.

"Legend has it," she says, "that when the moon is full, these two wake and fly."

"What else? What else does the legend say?" I ask in a near-whisper, remembering my strange dream, the air rushing between us.

"Here," she gestures, motioning for me to look more closely at the base.

I detect a barely discernible Gothic script. Seen another way, it might just as easily be scraggles of dead bark. I bend down to see, running my fingertips across the grain. Yes, there's something.

I'm on my knees. The letters are swimming around crazily in front of my eyes, in focus, out-of-focus, blurring....

"The legend lives on," continues the white-haired woman, puffing on her pipe, grinning a toothless grin. Slowly, anxiously, with a sense of deadly purpose, she recalls a scene from long ago.

It was late one night and had just begun to snow, she says, when the two women were rudely awakened by a band of ignorant, bloodthirsty villagers. The rumor that these two women were living as wife and wife was more than the mob could bear. Their home was destroyed, and the women were terrorized, pursued through the woods in their nightgowns. They ran till they could run no longer, then fell to the ground, terrified and exhausted.

But as the mob closed in around them, their ferocious dogs grew strangely silent. They shrank back, whining, refusing to go near the two.

Suddenly there appeared a winged being, shining so magnificently that the crowd drew back in terror. Speaking in a voice of thunder, it said:

"These are my children!"

Shielding the women with its radiance, the angel's eyes burned like suns. Towering over the trembling crowd, it roared:

"You shall not touch a single hair on their heads!"

With that, a bolt of lightning shot across the pitch-black sky, striking the ground so suddenly and with such great force that the mob stood blinded and dazed for several minutes. When the air had cleared, the women were gone, and all that remained was a charred, smoking tree stump, or a piece of stone, or a sculpture—no one was ever sure just what it was. But inside, the figures of the two lovers could easily be seen, with their heads thrown back, their eyes cast heavenward, their expressions serene.

"And yes, Missy, you betcha," winks the old woman. "They're still around. Mmm-hmm. You'll see them from time to time, gliding across the face of the moon, holding hands, way up there in the night."

☾ ☾ ☾

I careen back down the mountain headed for the phone at the little Exxon station, wild with excitement, anxious to relate this marvelous adventure to Eve.

But again, there's no answer. Concerned, I try Fran, her next-door neighbor, and get no answer there either. Thinking maybe they've gone to Mary's, I try there. All I get is the answering machine. I try Diane's. It rings three times and the answering machine kicks on. I'm just about to hang up when I hear my name on the recording.

"Sunny," says the voice of Diane, "please call—" and she recites a number I don't recognize, repeats it once more, and the machine clicks off. That's all.

I get a sharp, hollow feeling in my gut as I dial. The rain has stopped and the air is heavy and thick, as if someone has reached down and plunked an enormous bell jar over this particular segment of the world. It feels so isolated here, so remote. Insular. That's the word I'm looking for. It's almost as if—

"Renfield Memorial Intensive Care Unit," says a female voice, blasting me back to the present.

"Uh, yes, I'm trying to reach Diane Stafford please?"

"I'll page her," she says, putting me on hold.

Diane comes to the phone.

"Hey, what's the matter?" I ask, my voice trembling. "Somebody hurt?"

"Sunny, where are you?" she asks, sounding tired and gray.

"I'm still in the mountains. Why? What's wrong?"

"It's Eve."

The hollow feeling grips me. "What?"

"They're not sure. It's a virus of some kind. She's in a coma, Sunny."

My mind shuts off and I stare past me blankly, out across the gravel past the gas pumps, past the meadow filled with flowers, through the trees, beyond the mountains.

14

I drive for what seems an eternity and then spend the next four hours in ICU with Eve, unable to reconcile what has happened, unable to deal with the tubes in her nose, the IVs, the goddam catheter, the shitty fluorescent monitors sounding like grotesque finches chirping in somebody's warped idea of an electronic game....

Diane is here, and Mary Elgin, and Eve's dad, I think, along with everyone who has ever known Eve in her entire life, it seems, fanning in and out, in and out, while she lies in a coma and no one appears to have a clue what the hell is wrong....

When I come to my apartment to shower and change, Grandma Malone phones and says she's at the airport. Would I come pick her up? Sure, I say, in a daze. Halfway to the airport it occurs to me she has arrived out of the blue, without explanation.

I pull up to the main entrance and see her sitting on a bench by the door. I must've mentioned my new van because she gets up and hurries to the curb, an overnight bag on her arm. I reach over and open the door and she climbs in, peering at me over the tops of her sunglasses.

"You all right?" she asks, squeezing my hand.

"Grandma," I say, hugging her neck. "How did you know?"

"I woke up in the middle of the night and I knew something was terribly wrong—I was so afraid you'd been in an accident...."

I can't control my tears. Grandma's warm familiar fragrance, the security of her arms and the rich timbre of her voice have suddenly turned me to Jell-O.

☾ ☾ ☾

We have been to the hospital. Grandma meets some of my friends, and her presence in some strange way seems to strengthen us all. She and Fran even exchange a joke or two. I get the feeling that her sensing my trouble and flying here on a hunch has profoundly impressed them.

☾ ☾ ☾

"Is Eve your lover?" she asks me pointedly, downing her second Maker's Mark in the cocktail lounge across the street from the hospital.

"Yes," I say.

Grandma orders another drink for herself and a deluxe grilled cheese for me. In the heavy silence that follows, I know she's probably considering the situation from every conceivable angle. That's her way.

"Does Mom know you came to see me?" I ask, shredding a napkin.

"No," she says. "Your mother's in Japan."

Oh. Well of course she is, I think with a certain amount of bitterness.

"I'm glad you came," I manage to smile, feeling weak all over.

She reaches over wordlessly and touches my hand.

When we walk out of the lounge and onto the street a couple of hours later, I'm stunned to find that it's night.

☾ ☾ ☾

Dozing off on a chair in the waiting room, I'm suddenly back in the mountains, in the meadow with the white-haired stranger. Puffs of smoke rise like steam from the depths of the Loving Tree, and I'm made aware that a bird flying high above us is actually Eve. Body too sick to sustain her spirit, she has gone soaring, the old woman tells me. And I'm made to understand that Eve sees me, hears me, watches me from where she circles in the clear blue beyond.

When I wake, I slip down the hall to Eve's room. A nurse is just leaving. She and an aide have rolled Eve onto her side. When they have gone, I crawl up next to Eve and lie facing her. Even with her eyes closed, her expression is one of puzzlement, her brow creased, lips pursed as if ready to speak or be kissed.

"Eve," I whisper, "I know you can hear me. I want to tell you about the tree I found. When you're well I'll take you there. I know you're going to get well, Eve. I know you're going to come back to us.

"The tree is called the Loving Tree and I'm not really sure about what happened, or if I was dreaming, or what, but I'm pretty sure it was real."

And I tell her about the white-haired old woman who appeared out of the mist that morning. I tell her the legend of the Loving Tree as it was told to me by the stranger, a tale of two women who, each full moon, come to life and fly, their spirits free. I tell her about dreamcatchers.

"Come back, Eve," I beg, stroking her hand.

The room glows blue by the light of the monitors. Beside me, that bird called the soul rasps lightly in her deep sleep. From my pocket I take an ornate carving no bigger than my thumb and place it in her cool, dry palm, securely wrapping each of her fingers around it, just as the white-haired stranger had done to me on that strange and misty morning.

What might be just a trinket or a keychain is a miniature Loving Tree, perfect in every detail.

Omnia vincit amor, it says. Love conquers all.

☾ ☾ ☾

All night long someone has clung to my back, moaning and whining about the cold. At first I think it's Grandma, then realize Grandma's sleeping down the hall in Kim's bed.

I drift off, and hear it again.

"I'm cold," whispers a very familiar voice. "I'm freezing."

I sit up and reach for the light so abruptly that Bennington barks in alarm.

The third time it happens, I'm awakened from a deep sleep by icy fingertips brushing my back and shoulders.

"Help me," the voice implores.

The next morning, when Grandma and I go to the hospital, I take along Eve's favorite forest-green sweats and a pair of thick socks. When no one's around I pull back the sheet from Eve's motionless body, kissing her temple in the process.

She is wearing a flimsy hospital gown. I don't know how I'm going to get it off of her with all these shitty tubes and wires and things extending from her body.

I reach down to slip the sweatpants over her feet. It's like dressing a baby as I pull the bunched-up leg over the slender blue toes, the graceful arch of her foot unresponsive to my touch. The veins at her ankles look like indigo ribbons floating in a sea of porcelain.

I inch the pants up slowly.

"Excuse me. May I ask what you're doing?

I whirl to find Nurse Russell. I clear my throat, puff out my chest, and pull myself up to my full, glorious height of 5'3", highly indignant at being interrupted in the act of dressing my comatose lover.

"Eve's cold," I say, as haughtily as I can.

Russell's bright blue eyes betray nothing.

"She's cold," I repeat.

"I don't think so. She's running a temp."

I turn away and slip the thick, hand-woven socks on Eve's feet, pulling the elastic up and over the bottoms of her sweatpants so that no skin will be exposed. Her catheter tube protrudes crazily from the baggy waistband.

I'm not sure what to do next. There's no way to put the sweatshirt on over her head without undoing the IV and oxygen tubes, and I'm fairly certain this would violate some code, anyway.

So, I do what my Uncle Bud does.

I stand mutely, stupidly, like a sack of potatoes, and let Nurse Russell make the next move.

Like a showdown at the OK Corral, we stand facing one another. She regards me silently, uneasily, as if I were a toilet bowl about to overflow.

Minutes pass. I stand firm. Russell does nothing, says nothing. Russell doesn't even blink. My sack-of-potatoes routine doesn't seem to be working. Perhaps Nurse Russell is already acquainted with my Uncle Bud.

At last, she opens her mouth.

"I heard you the other night, you know," she says.

"Heard me? What are you talking about?"

"I was around the corner when you climbed up in bed with her."

"You were?"

"Yes. And I heard you telling the story."

Gracefully, almost imperceptibly, Nurse Russell moves to the bedside, begins undoing Eve's catheter, her IV and oxygen units.

"It was beautiful," she says. "Are you a writer?"

"Yes," I reply.

"Want to give me a hand here?" She motions toward the sweatshirt. "I'll lift her up, you slip it over her head, okay? One, two, three...."

When Grandma comes back by the room shortly afterwards, she nods wholeheartedly.

"I see you managed," she smiles.

She brushes a strand of Eve's hair from her forehead and takes my hand.

"Green's a good color for her, Sunny," she says. "See there? I think she's looking better already.

☾ ☾ ☾

It has been a long, strange day, and I have spent most of it here with Eve. It's about midnight. Friends started filling up the visitor's waiting lounge early this morning, and during the afternoon, Bradley, her dad, took everyone to lunch at Dearborn's.

Patty Euphoria says the reason we all like Bradley so much is that he's one of the girls. I guess it's true. Today, sitting beside him in the hospital lounge, I became intrigued with the cinnamon-amber hand-stitched calfskin loafers he was wearing. I must have been staring because he said—

"They're Italian. Like to try one on?"

And without thinking, I slid my foot down in the one he had just taken off. His feet are only a couple of sizes larger than mine. We chat about shoes, a personal love of mine, and his, apparently, for maybe half an hour.

I like Eve's father very much, but their resemblance—from their bony, delicate hands to their fine, straight noses and sparkling eyes—is unsettling. Their quiet voices and the way they turn a phrase, that sly little laugh.... Sometimes when we're talking it's as if I've known this man forever, then I realize it's his daughter I've known, and am suddenly left feeling deflated and empty, as if I'll never be totally at ease around him until Eve is well. Strangely, I sense in him the same reluctance towards me, so much invested, both of us loving her so much.

Classes begin next week, I realize with a sense of foreboding. Diane has been swamped with meetings, seminars, and faculty functions, so her visits to the hospital have been erratic. She sweeps into the room just now and goes directly to Eve, leans over, kisses her.

"Wake up, you lazy thing," she says, in a voice big with buffoonery. But she can't hide the pain, or the grief and exhaustion there.

"Any change?" she asks, turning to me.

"Her temperature is down some."

"That's good. How are you doing, kiddo?"

"Okay."

"Where's your grandma?"

"Off with Fran and Della somewhere."

She walks over and hugs me, and we stand holding each other for a very long time.

"You're too thin," she says with a frown. "Did you eat anything while you were on vacation?"

"Of course I did."

"The Sunny Calhoun nut and berry diet, huh? By the way, how WAS your trip? I never even asked."

"It was all right."

"Just all right?"

"Well, actually, parts of it were pretty incredible."

"Good. Now go eat. I want to hear all about it when you get back."

I slip down the hall to the lounge, sensing that Diane needs time alone with Eve. The pathologists as yet are still undecided regarding the exact nature of her condition. Whether it's a virus, an allergic reaction, or a toxic buildup of some kind, nobody's sure.

It's not just Diane who needs time alone with Eve.

Today as I passed by in the hallway, Bradley was sitting in Eve's cubicle, holding her hand. He was talking to her as if she were conscious, and he was telling her a story.

☾☾☾

Sometimes it works, sometimes not. Most of the time it doesn't. But I keep at it. I keep trying. As I drift off to sleep I tell myself, over and over, it's a dream and I'm dreaming. It's a dream and I'm dreaming. And if during a dream I happen to realize I'm dreaming, then I can remember whatever it is that I'm supposed to remember. It's self-hypnosis and it works. Sometimes. If I remember.

Shining iridescent in the moonlight, my dreamcatcher hangs on the wall above my bed. I take it and fan myself gently. Dreamcatcher, I whisper, please take me there. Please deliver me to that special twilight place I know.

...I'm running through a field of tall grass, my arms spread wide into the wind, and something, I'm not sure what, reminds me I'm dreaming. Maybe it's the all-over feeling of lightness, or my feet, which aren't touching the ground. Suddenly I know, and I'm filled with a sense of apprehension.

"Where are you?" I shout.

The wind stands still. Lightning flings its flares, and something, something in the orchard wanders among the trees.

"Where are you?" I call, hurrying out over the silky sea of night.

She appears from nowhere, smiling. She looks different somehow, older, fuller, but I know her and my heart leaps for joy.

"I'm here now," she says.

A radiance emanates from her. She folds me in her arms, caressing me, touching my face. I cannot recall why I'm crying.

I'm telling this to Mary Elgin. We're in her kitchen and she's fixing lemonade. The feeling that I truly visited Eve last night has been so powerful that I'm dazed, in an altered state all day.

Mary listens. And now she offers something else. Eve also paid her a visit in the night, she says.

They were in the lobby of a large hotel. As Mary was stepping into the elevator she was surprised to see Eve getting off. She was all dressed up. Heels, jewelry.

"Oh, Eve. We've all missed you so. Where have you been?"

Eve had only smiled. "Away," she had said, as the door was hissing shut. "Away on business."

15

Kim is back. When she arrives unannounced in the middle of the night and finds my grandma in her bed, she tiptoes down the hall and crawls in with me.

The rain has finally stopped and it's as if Kim has brought with her the lamp of daylight I've so badly needed. She lies next to me in the crazy morning light. Birds clamor and tweet outside my open window.

"They're welcoming you back," I say.

She brushes a tear from my eye.

"It's as if I've been on autopilot the past few days," I tell her. "Something went click in my brain that morning at the gas station when Diane told me about Eve. I think a part of me is still wandering around out there with a phone up to my ear."

A piece of me is missing, I say.

☾ ☾ ☾

Grandma's flapping around on the front porch when Kim and I get back from the store with breakfast.

"Where have you been?" she shrieks. "Diane called from the hospital half an hour ago. Eve's awake!"

☾ ☾ ☾

They've moved her out of ICU now and into a room on the seventeenth floor.

The pathologists mutter sternly, then retire for a game of golf.

"By and large," they pontificate, "it appears to be an intestinal disorder."

"Right. It's a fucking bullshit microscopic parasite," Eve affirms, high on pain killers. "By and large, not enough alcohol in my system, and God only knows what'll happen now if I quit smoking too! Somebody call Patty Euphoria!"

Diane rolls her eyes. "Sometimes a coma can be a good thing," she mumbles.

"And look at this," Eve yells, holding up her chart, waving it. "Under sex, they gave me an F! Geez, I didn't think I was *that* bad."

"Good God," says Diane, with a straight face.

"C plus," I nod.

"See what I have to put up with?" Eve implores, throwing her hands in the air.

Later, a nurse pops in, asks can we keep it down, we're disturbing the other patients.

"No, that's *four* margaritas, *two* gin-and-tonics, a Corona and a white wine," Eve tells her.

It's been like this all day.

☾ ☾ ☾

Eve has been resting, the pandemonium has died down. The pathologists have been muttering something about e coli bacteria. Sort of like food poisoning. She'll be released in another day or two. The nephrologists want to keep her under observation for a little while longer.

When I walk into her room tonight after everyone has gone, there is an aura I cannot explain. Part of me is afraid it's only a dream. Eve smiles up at me through half-closed eyes. I stand by the bed, disoriented. There is still an oxygen tube at her nose.

"It's so good to have you back," I say.

"Oh, but I never really left," she whispers.

☾ ☾ ☾

While we're waiting at the airport for her to board the plane for her return flight home, Grandma rubs some Jergens lotion on her hands, and I totally dissociate for a moment, because the faint coconut scent reminds me so much of Eve. I had never even realized it.

Grandma's telling me what it was like after Grandpa died. "I thought there'd never be anyone so dear, who understood me as well," she says.

I remember their house—deep rugs everywhere, Toulouse-Lautrec originals on the walls. I was five or six at the time. When Grandpa died of a stroke, Grandma started drinking and didn't let up till years later when she moved in with Aunt Buck, who wasn't really an aunt at all. Marie Buckingham was rough and audacious and owned about forty acres of downtown St. Paul. She pursued Grandma shamelessly.

"When I lost George," says Grandma, "I thought I'd lost everything. And in a way I guess I had."

Though it took her three years, Aunt Buck finally won Grandma.

Her eyes shine with emotion.

"Sunny," she says, holding me close. "No matter what happens in life, don't ever stop growing. Don't ever give up on love."

☾ ☾ ☾

It's her first night home from the hospital and I don't want to let Eve out of my sight. Olga shares my insecurity. She jumps up on the bed and lies purring between us, sounding just like a speedboat.

☾ ☾ ☾

Bradley has already gone to bed. He's catching an early flight back to San Francisco in the morning.

I decide to pay Mary a visit. Together we walk down the path, made narrow by creeping moss rose, to the flagstone patio behind her house, where we sip gin. Potbellied Larchmont investigates a nearby hedge.

"So, Mary," I clown, "is it true your body is now inhabited by the spirit of Eve's deceased mother, meaning, of course, that you are Bradley's ex-wife?"

"Right," she grins. "Walk-ins And Their Former Spouses—next Sally!"

"Is it true what everybody says? Is Bradley gay?" I ask.

"He thinks he is," she says elusively.

There's a ring around the moon tonight. It hangs just over my right shoulder. I lean back in my chair, staring up at the sky.

"You know the Milky Way is the path of souls," says Mary.

No, I say, I didn't know that.

☾ ☾ ☾

"Angels and wizards, wherever you go," smiles Kim. I have just finished telling her all about my vacation adventures. We're sprawled on the back porch, guzzling Singapore Slings, despite the fact that we both have early classes in the morning.

L.A. has been good to her, she says. She has a full-time

job lined up with the agency where she did her internship when she graduates in December. She and her boss are very close. That is, they phone each other two and three times a day. Being hundreds of miles apart is wrenching, she says.

Celia is her boss's name. As soon as Kim graduates, they plan to live together. Kim shows me a picture. Celia is stunning. She looks like Angelica Huston.

Interesting, we've both gotten involved with our bosses, Kim adds. Really. What are the odds of such a thing?

"Just a sound career move," I say, half-joking. Kim's career as an illustrator looks far more promising than mine right now. I don't even have a job. Eve has closed down the agency indefinitely.

"Are you going to move in with her?" Kim wants to know.

I'm torn.

"Do it," she urges. "If it were me, and I had the chance to live with Celia right now—" she doesn't finish, just smiles, puts her hand on my shoulder.

"Thanks," I say. "We'll see." But Kim and I have shared this house, this life, for four years. To move out now would seem wrong, somehow.

"Have you made any plans for after graduation?"

I sigh, shaking my head. It's all so nebulous, so up in the air.

"Come see us in L.A.!"

"Kim, you're a sweetheart." But I'm afraid I don't sound too enthusiastic.

"Still thinking about grad school?"

"Maybe. I don't know. Not right away. Eve and I have been talking about doing some traveling."

"Excellent! All I ask is a half-hour's notice before you show up on the doorstep."

I don't tell her it's Europe we're discussing. Neither do I

say how much I envy Kim her outlook, her future. I just can't seem to shake the feeling of trouble ahead.

"Hey," she says. "You crazy poets are all alike." She puts an arm around me, winks, lightly knocks her head against mine. "You worry too much."

I grin and shrug. Yeah, probably.

☾ ☾ ☾

It casts a long shadow across me in my bed. The dreamcatcher's intricate webbing glints in the moonlight as a gentle night breeze catches two yellow feathers extending from its base and rocks it slowly from side to side, back and forth rhythmically, back and forth like the hull of a ship in the arms of the sea. And I am slipping away, into a place of crowded dreams.

The wind howls all around me. It is an all-too-familiar sound. This is a square-rigger whaling ship going down, sinking fast. There's something I must remember to do if I can just think what it is and stay calm. The hull is splintering, the center mast breaks like a clap of thunder, we're swept from the deck, someone grabs my arm, calls me Sammy. This triggers something in my memory, but I'm not sure what. Stay calm, if this is a dream then it really isn't happening. Now the ice, now the shock, now the terrible...

If I have to swim for a hundred years I'll get back to you, back into your arms, somehow oh please, please, please...

☾ ☾ ☾

I run into Mary Elgin up at the liquor store.

"Come over," she says, delighted. "I want to show you my latest work."

She hops aboard her little pink scooter and roars up the winding avenues to her house, and I follow in the van.

We climb the stairs to her studio. She opens the door and we enter. Taking my hand, she guides me past a stack of easels, around a conglomeration of lawn chairs and hubcaps.

"Here," she says, standing before the east wall of her studio. "This is my latest project."

It's a mural. It's painted on the east wall of her studio, and it's at least twenty feet long. She has primed the entire thing with bright yellow gesso. All throughout, faces, scenes and houses stand out in storybook fashion. I recognize one figure as Eve, another is Diane. Over there is Sweet Jane, and beside her, Fran and Della and Snappy Pat and Suzanne and some people I hardly know, and there's even a miniature Dearborn's, downtown, and of all people, Grandma is coming out the door wearing her silk hat and glasses...and there I am, roaring along in my van, waving....

"Oh, Mary," I say, "this is absolutely wonderful."

"Thank you," she smiles. "I just started it last week, and there's plenty of wall space left, so if you have a particular story or memory you'd like me to include—"

"Mary, this is wonderful," I repeat. "It's like a family album!"

"Exactly," she says, pleased. "A scrapbook of our collective unconscious."

"Oh, and look, there's Patty Euphoria making a wine delivery! And there's Jones and Holly and—oh, Mary, *I love* this! What are you going to call it?"

"I'm calling it 'The Long Yellow Wall of Summer,'" she says.

☾ ☾ ☾

While she lay unconscious in the hospital, Eve explains, she relived much of a lifetime before.

"Look into my eyes," she says.

When I do, the noise of gulls and surf overpower me.

"Do you remember that house on the Cape in the rain," she asks, "and that room with the flowered wallpaper?"

"Yes."

The flames hiss and pop. I languish in her arms, just barely awake. Because it's a rainy night, we've made a fire in the fireplace and are stretched out in a drowse with Olga snoozing hugely between us and Bennington sprawled at our feet. We're lying in a nest of Hudson Bay blankets, wrapped in big, extravagant robes from Bradley, mine sage, hers emerald. Eve leans over, kisses me out of my stupor, undoes my robe. Still damp from a shower, tendrils of her hair brush my breasts and shoulders.

"Make you crazy?" she grins impetuously.

"No, not at all," I lie.

Her eyes sparkle down on me like jewels.

"I can remember you from before," she says.

The scene was Massachusetts, the late 1800s. A sea captain, a widower with a young son, remarries. I was the son, Eve was my stepmother, Diane my father.

"My feelings for you were not those of a mother," says Eve.

Do you remember, she asks? Do you remember?

I rearrange the blanket over her back, enjoying the pressure of her on my groin.

"I remember you with green eyes. And whiskers."

"Hmm. Was I a redhead?"

Yes, she nods. "And very young. You were a sailor."

"And you?" I ask, piqued.

"You don't remember?"

"Well, no, not exactly. Mostly I remember drowning."

"Yes," she nods slowly. "You were lost at sea."

"Come here," I say. My hands under her elbows, I ease her against me till we're face to face in the firelight.

It's almost as if I do remember: evenings by the hearth,

reading aloud to each other while he was long gone at sea, the light in her eyes....

On the other hand, this might be a fanciful game of karmic musical chairs. And I might be inclined to say so if the memories, the dreams, were any less vivid on my part.

Come all ye young sailormen, listen to me—
I'll sing you a song of the fish in the sea....

☾ ☾ ☾

I am looking out on the sea at high tide and the water looks like blue-black ink, and the moon dancing on the water looks like spilled white paint or pieces of white shell.

I look out at the moonlight through the wavy panes of my window and my breath makes a foggy patch on the glass. My hands and feet are numb with cold.

She comes up behind me silently, puts her hands on my waist, kisses me. Lifts my nightshirt slowly. Sinks to her knees, takes me in her mouth. We move clumsily to the bed. She pushes aside the heavy quilt and I lie down beside her...

I wake in a sweat to the sounds of Eve snoring. I shake her gently and she stops. Moonlight is pouring through the windows.

I close my eyes, and am back in that room again, the room overlooking the sea. She's next to me, her fingers slowly lifting the nightshirt above my head. She leads me from the beveled window to the bed. By the light of the moon I see that I am a boy. Maybe sixteen.

She takes me inside her. She's wet and hot and I keep sliding out, I'm shaking so. She laughs and takes me in her mouth. I'm going to be punished for this. Oh, God, I'm going to be struck dead. I'll burn forever in hell.

Above me on all fours, her hands under my hips, she spreads herself, takes me deep inside her, rocking back and forth. Wet, slishing sounds. Her breasts in my face.

Downstairs, a door slams. Heavy footsteps clomping up the stairs.

I wake to sunlight, disoriented. I lift the sheet quickly, and am relieved to find I'm myself again.

Eve wakens. Our eyes meet. She takes my hand. Kisses it.

"I was dreaming about you," she whispers.

"Me too."

"Tell me."

"You were..."

"Yes?"

"Having your way with me," I reply, uncertainly.

"Yes," she smiles. "Nice, wasn't it?"

"Very."

She reaches down, slides her hands under my panties. "Tell me about it."

"We were...it was in a room, in a house, by the sea."

"Yes."

"And you came upstairs and—"

"And what?"

"I think you already know."

"Faster?" she whispers.

"No, slower."

"Sorry."

"You seduced me."

"Yes? Can you be a little more specific?"

"I was..."

"Hmmm?"

"...you were..."

"Yes?"

"Can't. I'm gonna—"

"No you're not." She pulls her hand away.

"Eve! That's not fair."

Grinning, she kisses me, starts in again.

"We were having the same dream, Sunny."

"Are you sure it was a dream?"

"Past-life recall, then."

"Seems like it...ohhh there...it was pretty good, wasn't it?"

"Yes," she whispers, kissing me. "It was."

"I think I like this life better."

"Why?"

"Less seamy. Without the guilt. Eve, I can't do this much longer—"

"Good," she says. "Say it."

"You feel so good," I breathe.

"Say it," she says, searching deep in my soul.

"Ohhh..."

"Say it." She's shaking my very bones.

"I love you I love you."

"I love you, Sunny," she whispers, and then I lose track of time, of where she ends and I begin, of what's her and what's me, for looking into her eyes all I can see is her looking back at me and me back at her and on and on and on, forever, infinity.

We just keep making love all morning and I miss all my classes and by two in the afternoon we're exhausted and so we send out for lunch. We shower and lie in bed feeding each other and Eve tells me what she can remember of our past life, and I listen, completely absorbed.

She tells me how she relived parts of it, unconscious in the hospital, as if it were a dream she had dreamed before.

"Is there some way we could check this out, have it verified?" I wonder.

"I'm sure we could," says Eve. "But would that really prove anything? Would it make our feelings for each other any more real?"

"Well, no, I suppose not," I say, getting her point.

☾ ☾ ☾

She ran an alehouse in New Bedford in the mid-1800s. Her name wasn't Eve then of course, it was Katrina; she was known as Kate. A lusty, brawling widow, she owned the Blue Lantern Inn, a waterfront dive frequented by whalers, cut-throats and other ruffians. Of her regulars, when he wasn't off to sea, Captain Dan was her favorite, and by far her most generous client.

Soon after the death of his frail, aristocratic wife, leaving behind a moody, bewildered twelve-year-old son, the dashing, reckless Captain Dan remarried. The news of society's handsomest and most sought-after man pairing with the likes of Kate Bennigan caused quite a scandal, and shock waves were felt all the way to Boston.

But the years passed, and the rumors subsided, and their elegant Georgian home took on new vigor and respectability and two more children were born. The once-despondent Sammy, under his stepmother's influence, grew into a scholarly, likeable young man.

When a third child was born, however, whispers began anew, for Captain Dan had long been gone to sea. This delicate, fine-boned child bore a striking resemblance to young Sam, then barely eighteen.

Shortly after Captain Dan's return from a lengthy and highly successful whaling voyage, the course of Sammy's life was forever altered. Instead of attending Harvard as he had hoped, he found himself Arctic-bound, an unwilling crew member aboard one of his father's square-rigger fishing vessels.

Captain Dan stayed home with his wife and children, and within the year, Sammy was drowned at sea.

"I begged him not to send you, I begged and begged."

☾ ☾ ☾

I finish the last of our pizza in silence.

"Who do you suppose we'll be in our next life, Eve?" I ask.

She smiles, shaking her head.

"Well, maybe we should plan this thing out, Eve. Do we want children? Do you like me better male or female?"

Her laughter sounds like water running in a forest.

"It doesn't matter, Sunny," she says, pulling me close. "Just as long as we're together."

16

A six-pack of Watney's stout and a kitchen full of bread dough and I'm happy. I'm up to my elbows in flour and have on this really snazzy baker's apron Grandma bought me. The radio's on to my favorite classical station—it's a ritual when I bake. I'm doubling the recipe so there'll be loaves for Fran and Della, Diane and Marcy, Mary Elgin, Kim, maybe Pat.

It's a very time-consuming recipe with different stages and lots of waiting, but the end result is a whole-grain bread with the lightness and consistency of angelfood cake. I do this maybe once a year.

I hear the front door, so Eve must be back from her appointment. I hear her keys jangling, the rustle of coat, the thud as Olga jumps down from the window and hurries over to greet her, the clatter of approaching footsteps as her nose leads her into the kitchen.

"Mmmm," she murmurs, standing watching me in the doorway.

"Mmm-*hmmm*," I wink, blowing her a kiss. She looks ravishing in linen pants and an apricot silk blouse that slashes downward between her breasts. "Come here and give me a hug."

She does. She comes up behind me and puts her arms around my waist, presses herself against my back. She holds me like this, her chin on my shoulder.

"What cha drinking?"

"Stout," I say. "Wanta taste?"

She takes the bottle, studies it judiciously. "Never heard of it." She takes a hefty swig. She swigs some more. "Hmm." She sets the bottle down on the counter top, her pelvis bumping me rhythmically.

"How'd it go at the doctor's?"

"Elaine and Judie are going on a women's cruise in January."

"Oh? How nice."

Dr. Elaine Connor has been a friend of Eve's since her travel agency days.

Eve watches as I pop two more loaves in the oven. When I turn back to her there are tears in her eyes. She takes my hand and holds me close.

"Sunny," she says, "I love you."

We stand like that for what seems like forever, and then she tells me.

"No," I say firmly, "It's got to be a mistake. Somebody goofed. It happens all the time in labs. Make them test you again, Eve."

Please, I beg her, make them test you again.

"They already have," she says. This was her third time.

☾ ☾ ☾

I spend the next few days wandering in all directions, the light and warmth of summer seeming to slip away through this rip in the fabric of my life. To make sense of it would be like trying to catch a tempest in a net.

I come to Blue Cliff Hill. A west wind is blowing, the world falls away. I hear only the pound of my heart.

☾ ☾ ☾

Full-blown AIDS.

I don't know quite what I was expecting, really, or why

it came as such a shock. We knew it was a possibility. No, be honest, we knew it was inevitable. Somehow, I guess I hoped that when she quit drinking and gave up smoking and started on the mega-vitamin/amino acid supplements, it might improve her chances...

But the intestinal virus has pushed her over the edge.

Bradley arrived the next day. This time, there were no golf games with the other doctors, no happy hours at Dearborn's. This time, Bradley took his last surviving family member, his daughter, and they left on a jet for Mexico. They were gone for a week.

☾ ☾ ☾

When she comes back we go to the hills on a picnic to enjoy the fall colors and to find time alone.

Butterflies and sunflowers riot in the fields. Bees hover nearby. Late-afternoon sunlight makes us drowsy as old she-bears preparing for long winter naps. Eve lies with her head in my lap, eyes closed, a plaid blanket thwarting the chill that plagues her constantly these days.

"It's been like getting to know you all over again," I tell her. No head buried in a sea of computer printouts, no billowing clouds of cigarette smoke all around you, no hangovers anymore. I'm becoming reacquainted with a very tender person who's been hiding behind a screen of paperwork for many years.

A sudden breeze passes over our hillside, whisking the tops of trees nearby. I fall silent, and she reaches for my hand. Both of us smile, and the air tingles with the sounds of contentment.

☾ ☾ ☾

She has her good days and her bad days now, with nothing in between. One day she rallies, the next she is ill.

On bad days, it's as if I've watched Eve age twenty years. On a bad day she's morose and forgetful and doesn't bother getting dressed.

Sometimes, on a good day, we catch a glimpse of the old Eve, the wild, fiery Eve everybody loves, and the house fills up with the ring of laughter, and it's summertime all over again.

From day to day there's no way of knowing what to expect, only that she grows thinner, and more pale. Thanksgiving comes and goes.

☾ ☾ ☾

To be honest, I don't remember very much about my graduation, but that it was freezing cold and snowing that night and the auditorium was packed and everyone's face looked green under the bright hot lights, and the ceremony seemed endless and Kim and I sat together, both of us drunk, having to pee really bad.

My family was there and so was Kim's; Diane, Eve and Marcy came and everybody sat together. Before the ceremony, all of us had dinner downtown at a Chinese place and Grandma broke the ice by noting how much better Eve was looking since the last time she saw her.

"Yeah," quipped Diane, "she wasn't wearing any clothes then."

"Right," Eve deadpanned. "Most people wouldn't even notice the difference."

Mother sat next to Diane and all through dinner I couldn't help thinking what a lovely couple they'd make, and only a few years difference in their ages...

After the reception at my parents' hotel, Kim and I excused ourselves and went slinking off to a bar of low repute. We ended up at an all-night party at the home of one of her ex-lovers. Might as well break the fun barrier, I reasoned, after all, it's Christmas, I've just graduated from college, my lover is dying and I have absolutely no plans for the future.

At dawn Kim and I hitched a ride back home in somebody's beat-up Pathfinder and I threw up in the yard.

☾ ☾ ☾

In the morning, Eve is exhausted, and so am I. Yesterday has taken its toll. She can barely stand up, much less make it to the bathroom without assistance.

"I was afraid of this," she grimaces as she lies back down.

"Just rest," I say, holding her hand.

"It's so damn frustrating," she frets. "So humiliating."

A tear makes its way down her cheek. She looks fragile. As fragile as glass.

The phone rings and it's Grandma calling from the hotel. We had all planned on going shopping today. When I explain that Eve has overextended herself, I hear Aunt Buck in the background, heartily volunteering to come over and look after Eve.

"You all run along," I hear her say. If I didn't know better I'd think Aunt Buck had a crush on my lover.

Mom, Dad, Jim, Grandma and I shop all morning and have lunch about forty stories up in a skyscraper. The restaurant is dark and hushed and filled with suits, not the kind of place you'd want to just kick back and order a Colt 45 or a Schlitz malt liquor, which is really what I'd like to have. I settle for a Lowenbraü.

It's almost Christmas Eve and the place is a madhouse. Grandma goes over and chats with her old buddy Wilson, the maitre d'. One of the waiters flirts with my brother. People are always flirting with Jim.

When Dad crosses his legs I can see that he's wearing one black sock and one brown, but at least his loafers match.

Mom orders a Jack Daniels on the rocks with a beer back, and another, then asks me which graduate schools I've been considering.

☾ ☾ ☾

Her arm is thin and white, her wrist almost transparent. Smiling, Eve reaches out to me as I climb into bed.

"I missed you," she says.

We snuggle. We kiss. She tells me about her day. She and Aunt Buck built a bird feeder.

A what?

"You know. A bird feeder. Aunt Buck went rummaging through the garage and found a bunch of old lumber. It's so cute, Sunny. Little shingles on the roof and everything."

"Where is it? Can I see?"

"Oh, we left it out back till the paint dries. I'll show you in the morning. And how was your day?"

I relate the trauma of Christmas shopping, lunch at Wentworth's. She rests her head in the curve of my shoulder, listening, stroking my hair.

☾ ☾ ☾

They would have stayed a couple of days longer but the weather got so bad that their flight back home was nearly cancelled. Another foot of snow fell during the night and an ice storm is on its way. Nothing feels good or right about my family leaving so soon after Christmas.

I can tell Eve is in a lot of pain. All day long she sits next to the window, dozing fitfully, wringing her hands beneath the blanket.

☾ ☾ ☾

Kim wants to be in L.A. by New Year's. She's rented a U-Haul and has it hooked to the back of her little green Honda and most of her stuff is packed—all the good stuff, like her blue recliner, the pecan bookcases and the stereo system. The house really looks bare. Bennington's nervous and depressed. She loves Kim as much as I do.

But first things first. Kim can't leave until tomorrow because Diane has orchestrated a going-away party for her over at Mary Elgin's. Diane and Marcy have just returned from their Costa Rican cruise, and they've been fighting. The atmosphere is tense. They give me a pink and green striped t-shirt with some big-billed birds roosting in palm trees on the front.

"Thanks," I say, slipping it on, loving that new smell.

Diane wants to know if I'm going to continue renting the apartment now that Kim's moving out, or am I going to move in with Eve?

I don't know. Haven't decided. I'd miss having you across the alley, I tell her.

Diane and Marcy disappear into the bedroom to argue some more, so I take the opportunity to call Eve, to tell her about this party for Kim tonight.

Eve's feeling a little better. She's editing some more of my stuff. If she takes a nap she can probably make the party, she says.

"See you in my dreams," she says.

"Yes," I say, and hang up, recalling that a few nights ago both of us had awakened at the same time. We had been dreaming about flying, holding hands, soaring high above green and gold and auburn hills.

☾ ☾ ☾

The party is a real bash but I can't bear to think of Kim leaving. She starts crying, and so do I.

"You'll just have to come to L.A.," she repeats, and we hold each other in a quiet hallway away from the crowd. As I stroke her pale spikey hair and gaze into those smoke-colored eyes, it occurs to me that Kim may be my daughter from another life.

But I don't say this, only "I love you, I'll miss you,"

feeling lately as if all of us, everywhere, have been shot from cannons, our lives accelerated nearly to the speed of light.

"I want to show you something," I say, and taking her hand I lead her up the steep narrow stairway to Mary's studio. Then, crossing to the side of the hall that leads to her screened-in workroom, I open the door and switch on the lights.

It is freezing out here. Mary has moved most of her painting supplies inside for the winter. All that remains are some old scraps of lumber, a sculpture or two, some odds and ends. And, of course, The Wall.

There, like an action-packed adventure movie, busier and fuller than a dream, is the mural.

"Oh my God!" exclaims Kim, trying to assess this life-document. "My God," she repeats, raising her arms as if in supplication, her breath a misty vapor.

"Sunny, this in unbelievable!" she beams. She points to a skater threading her way along the river, on a path through the woods. "Is that me?"

"Yes. And here you are again on the back porch wolfing pie."

"Is that Eve?" Kim asks. "But what's that in her hands?"

"Her dreamcatcher," I reply.

"Oh, yeah, the dreamcatcher. Say, does that thing really work?"

"It all depends," I say. "If you believe that it does, then it does."

She searches my eyes deeply.

Both of us start to shiver. We're without coats and it's about 10 degrees out here. We edge towards the door.

"I've been told you can hear music inside the painting if you listen long enough. I have, I think," I say.

Beside me, her eyes wide and sparkling, Kim listens.

"Nah. All I hear is silence," she testifies, after a considerable pause.

"It's not silence," I whisper. "It's the sound of time."

☾☾☾

Kim is leaving, going home to a new job, a new lover, and probably a very rewarding new career. Her faded green Honda sits packed and ready for the trip. It's a beautiful day for a trip, the air clear and cold and the sky brilliant turquoise.

We sit amidst the clutter of breakfast, lingering over coffee. I have fixed strawberry crepes, her favorite.

"If you ever need a break from writing," she says, smacking her lips, "you'll be doing the world a favor by becoming a pastry chef."

"Thanks," I tell her. "That reminds me, I want to send along some of that bread with you. And there's a pie, too. To keep your strength up."

"Sunny, I love you. You're too much." She hugs my neck. "And I've got a little something I want to give you, too." She hands me a flat box, wrapped in banana-yellow tissue paper.

"What's this?"

My heart pounds and my fingers flutter as I open the package.

It's a photograph in a beautifully matted frame. But no, it only *looks* like a photograph. It's so precise and detailed it fooled me at first. It's a hand-painted picture and it's of Kim and me, barefoot, windblown and smiling, arms around each other, out on the rickety wooden steps of the porch on the farm.

"I remember this," I say, my eyes clouding with tears.

"Yeah. I used that ratty old photo Carla took of us with her Instamatic, and I drew this enlarged copy. Then I painted it with prismacolors."

It was late spring our first year at Renfield, a cookout at the farm after a game, and Kim has captured our wildness, our exuberance.

"I can almost smell the lilacs blooming," I say, staring. "Kim, this is a treasure."

"I'm glad you like it," she says. "I did make one minor change that wasn't visible in the original photograph. See it?"

"Yes," I say, reaching for her, holding her close. "Thank you."

"Remember that," she says.

What Kim had added, whisper-thin and shining, was the silver thread of love extending from our hearts.

☾ ☾ ☾

Diane has invited about 400 of her closest friends to her New Year's Eve party. There are lots of new faces here, musicians, symphony people, friends of Marcy. Some are from out of town.

It's a casual affair. Diane is in Levis and a flannel shirt and Marcy looks adorable in her new designer sweats with the tiny muscle-bound dyke on the sleeve and chest. Diane ordered them from San Francisco. They're a soft shade of apricot with khaki trim. Eve wants a pair.

A bunch of us are in the kitchen telling stories. Marcy's had quite a bit to drink and she forgets the punch line of her joke. But hearing the story that led up to it in Marcy's erratic, rapid-fire, brain-fever delivery with her frantic, sweeping gestures and her honey-rich Virginia accent is such an absolute delight that nobody cares in the least.

It's very late and the place is a shambles. Leftover food is strewn everywhere. Eve and Patty Euphoria are listening to the Supremes and Eve is sprawled in Patty's lap. There's bean dip in her hair. Mary Elgin appears to be engaged in rapturous conversation with Holly Kaufman.

Jones, Snappy Pat and I have been playing poker. Jones goes to the refrigerator for more beers and I get up to use the bathroom. But the little bathroom off the kitchen has gotten locked from inside and nobody can get the door open, and somebody's taking a shower in the master bath, so I cruise up the stairs to the second floor.

From down the hallway I hear moaning in the guest room. The door is partway open as I pass by. There's just enough light to distinguish two figures on the bed.

One of them is Mindy Ruffin, Channel 3, local news anchor. Mindy is having the time of her life.

And so, it appears, is Diane.

17

Most of the time, my apartment stands empty. Since Kim has gone it seems insane to be paying so much rent on a space I seldom use, and yet like an old friend, it's there for me. It is a sanctuary, a neutral zone, a place of refuge.

February. Unseasonably mild. Blue sky. Diane has suggested I paint her guest room, and so I do. The walls are drying now, the windows open to let in fresh air. Sunlight streams through the floor-to-ceiling glass as I stand amidst drop-cloths and canvas spread out on the varnished hardwood floor. The walls glow warmly in the fading afternoon light.

I am surveying my work when Diane walks in. She has just come from school. She appraises the room with a smile, an emphatic nod of her head. When she takes off her glasses there are deep circles under her eyes. She slips out of her jacket, kicks off her shoes. Most of the furniture has been shoved out of the room. The bed has been pushed toward the center and is piled with books and lamps and papers. Brushing aside the debris, Diane stretches out on the bed with a sigh.

"You did a nice job," she tells me. Her eyes come to rest on the top of my head.

"Come here," she says.

I replace the lid on a gallon of paint. Brush in hand, I cross over to her.

"There's paint in your hair," she grins.

"Yeah. I know."

Gazing up at me with eyes the deep mottled autumnal color of polished tortoise, she pats the space beside her.

Wearily, I join her.

She rolls onto her side and presses herself to my back and we lie like that, in the sun, and she strokes my hair.

"She's not getting any better," Diane tells me, as if it were news.

The minutes pass in silence, and I sense her heavy heart.

She's not getting any better. It's as if the enormity of Eve's illness has finally sunk in, leaving her helpless and paralyzed.

☾ ☾ ☾

Valentine's Day.

Diane gives Marcy a diamond. Eve gives me a gold watch. I give Eve a dozen red roses. And we all live happily ever after.

Diane fixes a celebration dinner. Creole something-or-other. Gumbo this and that. Hot and spicy. Delicious.

Afterwards we stretch out in the TV room, two to a sofa. We watch *Throwdown*, a suspenseful Lesbian-Ninja warrior-action video. I drink lots of beer. Eve falls asleep in my lap.

Marcy keeps holding her pudgy little hand up to the light, admiring her new ring. It's about two and a half carats.

☾ ☾ ☾

Yesterday was my birthday and today is the first day of spring.

Eve has a nurse now. Her name is Betty. Betty is an old friend of Eve's neighbor Fran, who's a retired nurse.

When Betty pulls up to the house in a Winnebago, I am impressed. The camper is so huge it fills one lane of the street and totally blocks the drive. My van looks like a toy beside her big rig.

Eve is still asleep. When Betty comes inside we have coffee and chat about her travels. This summer she'll be touring the Alaska Highway again.

Eve wakes and while Betty bathes her I putter in the kitchen, bake some cinnamon rolls. As I putter, robins and cardinals and a black-capped chickadee sing in the trees at the side of the house, and some loudmouthed bluejays zoom in to inspect the cheery red and purple bird feeder Eve and Aunt Buck made at Christmas.

I stand at the sink and gaze out the window. The thermometer on the other side of the glass reads fifty degrees and the clouds are clearing. The trees are budding and the wind is calling my name. Along the side of Fran and Della's house next door, the daffodils are in bloom like a wall of yellow silk.

Eve is sitting up in bed wearing a salmon-colored gown. Betty is brushing her hair and Eve stares at the TV, which is not on. She breaks into a smile as I enter the room and as she reaches for me I'm struck by the spontaneous childlike quality of her gesture. Her skin smells clean and powdery like a baby's.

"Feeling any older?" she wants to know.

Yesterday, Diane had thrown a small birthday party for me. There was an angelfood cake with twenty-four candles. The commotion was a little much for Eve. After everyone had gone I lay down beside her. She held me and spoke dreamily of a rooftop in Paris, Sangria mixed with vodka.

Yes, Eve, I tell her, I do feel older.

☾ ☾ ☾

Diane dropped by Eve's this morning and helped me with some housework. The place was kind of a wreck. There were ruined pans on the stove, charred and blackened from when I'd fallen asleep on the couch. A stray cat and her litter of kittens had moved in on the back porch. Bennington had been out scavenging and was sick with diarrhea. The trash hadn't been emptied for some time and there was laundry piled everywhere.

Okay, so maybe I had lost track of time a little, but only because I've been writing nonstop. Despite her fatigue, Eve's genius for editing is sharper than ever, and together we fill page after page with ideas, images, verses, stories, visions...

Last week we worked on a screenplay, several poems, a one-act play, and the outline for a short novel. These have been the most productive weeks of our relationship.

☾ ☾ ☾

Thursday afternoon. Eve's lying in bed stretched out for a nap, the remains of lunch on a tray beside her. She hasn't eaten much, but she rarely does nowadays. Most of the chicken I cut into bite-size morsels is still resting on her blue china plate. Maybe one or two bites are gone.

"Delicious," she nodded, then she was full. "Has anyone been in?" she wants to know. "Has Kenny been by for his proofs?"

"No, Eve." I remind her that the agency has been closed for several months now.

"Oh," she sighs, eyes momentarily clouding. Then, brightening, she asks me to tell her a story, and I start in, again, about the mountains, the Loving Tree, my vacation. She can never seem to hear enough of it.

She leans back, closes her eyes, and a wide smile transforms her features as I describe riding horseback through the wilderness that morning with Maggie, gathering branches for the dreamcatcher.

At this point she sits up, positively radiant.

"Let's go there!"

"Whaaaat?"

"Can we? Can we please?" Her grip on my hand tightens in anticipation.

Well, if we left early tomorrow morning we could be

there by afternoon, I suppose....

"I want to meet Maggie and Karen," she beams, "and I want to visit the Loving Tree.

"Maybe we could stay the weekend, come back Monday..."

Just then we hear, "Yoo hoo! Anybody home?"

Diane peeks in, arms loaded with groceries. "Hi ya, kids," she grins. "Anybody want ice cream?" She winks, heads for the kitchen. We can hear her in there clinking around, rattling spoons.

She returns carrying clear glass bowls loaded with Eve's favorite, Vanilla Swiss Almond.

"Yum," I say, reaching for mine.

"Look, Eve." Diane sits down on the edge of the bed, feeding herself and Eve. Eve takes a few bites and then begins drifting off. Reaching over, Diane squeezes her hand. "Sweet dreams, baby," she says, kissing her forehead.

We get up and come to the kitchen.

"Thanks for doing the shopping," I say gratefully.

"You doing all right?"

"Yeah, fine. We were just talking about a trip to the mountains when you came in."

Diane looks at me skeptically.

"She really wants to go," I say.

She takes another spoonful of ice cream, continues to stare.

"I think it's a good idea," I say.

She doesn't even blink.

"So I think we're going to leave in the morning."

Diane gives me one of her I'm-not-even-going-to-consider-this looks.

"Want some more?" she asks, holding up the carton.

"Yes."

"And how are you planning on getting there?" she asks, dishing out the ice cream.

"I'll drive."

"Do you think she's strong enough for such a long ride?" It's a rhetorical question.

"I'll fix her a bed in the back."

"And what if she gets sick, Sunny? Have you given this any thought?"

I stare at the floor.

"I know it would mean a lot to you. But I just don't think it's a very wise idea right now, Sunny."

"But...Diane. If not now—when?" I ask, my eyes brimming.

"Listen to me," she says, taking my face in her hands, looking hard into my eyes. "I'm sorry," she says, folding me in her arms.

☾ ☾ ☾

In the morning we go. A loudmouthed bluejay flaps noisily from branch to purple branch of the redbud tree as I'm loading the van.

Eve is wearing her white sweatpants. Even though they're size small, she's practically lost in them. She's awake and alert for the entire trip. We take back roads, driving slowly, saying little, enjoying the signs of spring.

By mid-afternoon we're in the mountains. Eve rolls down her window and breathes deeply. Bennington pricks up her ears as we swing down the shortcut road to Valley of the Clouds.

I chatter on wildly about Maggie and Karen's cozy, enchanted little hideaway in the pines, becoming more and more excited by the minute.

"I hope they don't mind us dropping in unannounced," Eve says.

"Don't worry," I grin. "I've brought five gallons of Bluebird wine."

But when we reach the village and I wheel into the yard

of the little blue cabin, everything looks different, everything looks changed. Gone are the old Dodge, the overturned washtubs, and the blown-out mattresses. Karen's yellow and white Bronco is nowhere in sight. Instead, a bulky, menacing Harley-Davidson straddles the porch. When a snarling, yapping pack of huskies race from the house and surround the van, Bennington begins to howl.

Eve looks over at me in confusion. I shrug. I park the van. Neither of us moves.

The curtain flutters and the cabin door squeaks open. A large woman moves slowly onto the porch. The woman does not call off her dogs. She wears greasy, faded overalls with no shirt. Around her head is a red bandanna. In her arms rests a shotgun.

"Good God," exclaims Eve. "She must think we're the revenuers." She turns to me with a sly smile. "Shall I ask if she has any Grey Poupon?"

I giggle in spite of myself. It's a scene right out of *Tobacco Road.*

"Excuse me," I call to the woman, trying to be heard over the uproar of dogs. I wave feebly. "I'm sorry to bother you but—"

KA-BOOM!

The woman raises her shotgun and fires into the air. The dogs are silenced at once. Cringing, they hurry from the van and crawl back under the porch.

"Yow!" I yelp, reaching for the ignition. "Let's get out of here!"

"Wait, Sunny," Eve says. "She's hollering something."

The large woman rests her gun on the railing and takes a few steps toward us.

"Excuse me," I say, summoning the courage to try again. "We're looking for Maggie and Karen?"

The woman's stern face lights up.

"You wouldn't be Sunny, would you?" she asks, drawing near.

"Yes, I am," I answer, sounding very much surprised.

"But who are you, and how did you know?"

"Val Bigfire," she booms, extending her hand. "Nice to meet you." Her voice is deep and rolling.

"This is my friend Eve," I say.

Val greets Eve and says, "You know, Maggie had a feeling you'd come. She and Karen are over at Black Hawk this week for Spring Festival. They had a dream you were on your way and asked me to escort you to the powwow if you showed up."

Eve and I exchange looks.

"Come on in," Val urges, reaching for my door. "You both look starved. I'll fix you some lunch."

☾ ☾ ☾

Like Maggie and Karen, Val has lived in these mountains all of her life. Spring Festival, she tells us, is not just another art and craft show. More importantly, it's an opportunity for locals to unwind and celebrate the passing of another long, hard winter. The powwow, a Native American ceremony and social get-together, is a part of that celebration. It is held for two nights during Spring Festival, and Anglos are welcome.

"Maggie's gonna be so happy to see you," says Val. "She just knew you'd make it."

When I tell her that I haven't talked to Maggie in more than six months, she only shrugs.

"Maggie knows what she knows," she says.

Val is a forest ranger. She and her dogs have just come off a six-week tour of Mount Shavano, and she's house-sitting for Maggie and Karen over Spring Festival. In her easy, robust way, she laughs and apologizes for what must have seemed a very hostile introduction.

"I'm just not used to being around people much," Val explains.

Following a hearty lunch and a peaceful nap, Eve and I are refreshed and restored. Towards evening we head down the mountain for Black Hawk. Val leads the way on her enormous black and silver Harley. The skies have turned dark and cloudy. Thunder rumbles through the valley. Eve is in good spirits. Neither of us has been to a powwow before.

In Black Hawk we can hear the powwow drums long before we've reached the fairgrounds. Boom-ba-boom, boom, boom. The top of my head starts to tingle. I park the van in an open field alongside hundreds of pickups, Jeeps, and horse trailers. A jagged bolt of lightning rips through the sky, followed by distant thunder. Several fat raindrops splat against the windshield.

"Hmmm," I mutter ominously.

"Don't worry," says Eve, her eyes luminous.

"Are you sure you're up to this?"

"Positive," she says.

We agree to keep it short. Thirty minutes tops. At the most, forty-five. I zip the zipper on Eve's warm parka, and help her with her mittens.

As we pass through the entrance gate, participants in a ceremonial dance hurry by, bells jangling, their costumes a blaze of color. Eve leans on Val's arm, her eyes wide. The aroma of cedar and sage wafts through the soft evening air.

Val strides powerfully ahead through the crowd, her chest held high, chin lifted. She leads us to Maggie Two Tree's pottery booth, where incredibly beautiful teapots, mugs, and dishware line the shelves.

Maggie beams when she sees us. Jumping up, she reaches out and we embrace. There are tears in her eyes. It is clear by the look we exchange that she knows about Eve.

Karen wanders by, her arms piled with rattles, beads, and feathers. She is without crutches, her broken leg mended. Seeing us, she gives a little whoop, does a little dance, and joins in our embrace. Another flash of lightning fills the sky.

The drums start up again. Maggie, Karen, and Val converse quietly in a language I don't understand. Val nods, disappears into the crowd as if on a mission, and shortly returns. In her hands she carries a walking stick.

Maggie takes the stick and places it in Eve's hands. We know that it is special.

"A gift from Mad Ida," says Maggie, motioning towards the old woman in a booth nearby. "Our Medicine Woman."

A few yards away, surrounded by ornately hand-carved walking sticks of every description, Mad Ida finishes her cigarette. A breastplate of bones covers her torso, and she wears a porcupine headdress.

For a second, Eve is caught off guard. She looks admiringly at her walking stick, then at Maggie and Karen, and back at Mad Ida. Catching Mad Ida's eye, Eve waves. Mad Ida nods and waves back. Eve calls out her thanks to the old woman, but Mad Ida only shrugs, no big deal.

When Eve blows her a kiss, the old woman bows, grinning a toothless grin, and her dark eyes sparkle.

☾ ☾ ☾

With one hand on my arm and the other securely on her hickory stick, Eve and I wander from booth to booth, and from tent to tent. With each beat of the drum, our spirits dance. Brilliant flashes of lightning illuminate our faces. Thunder rumbles and the air is filled with pulsating energy. A woman in buckskin begins a high-pitched chant.

We stop at the food tent for Indian tacos. They are crispy and delicious. Eve wolfs down three while I have one. Like a hyperactive child, she refuses to slow down, wants to do everything, and somehow we've gotten separated from our friends. Val is nowhere in sight. We merge back out into the stream of people to look for her.

As we near the Storyteller's Circle, I pause. At the center

of the circle I recognize the wise, handsome face of Juanita Claw. Juanita is head librarian over in Valley of the Clouds. She's a close friend of Maggie's.

Juanita is enthroned on a striped lawn chair atop several brightly woven rugs or shawls. An array of feathers hangs from her sash. Her hands outline images as she speaks, and her voice comes to me as softly as wind through cottonwood trees. Juanita's eyes, black as crow wings, penetrate the night. It is as if she speaks from a dream.

Eve and I find our places on a sturdy log. The little girl beside us doesn't glance up when we sit down, so absorbed is she by Juanita's story. She reminds me of myself at age four or five, enchanted by my grandma's magical tales.

Dozens of eyes are riveted on the silvery-haired woman as she sways gently from side to side, raising her hands to the sky.

"We call forth fruitful life," she says.

"We call forth fruitful life," repeat the listeners in unison.

Juanita moves her arms back and forth as she paddles an imaginary canoe through still waters.

"The human family is much like the salmon," she says. "All come forth from the lake of clear mind into the Ocean of Experience."

Imitating Juanita, the children paddle industriously.

"Like the salmon," Juanita says, "we have entered the stream leading to the source of our being. Just like the salmon, we are looking to find our way home."

In this great Ocean, she says, with its lessons and opportunities, we bump into one another. There are many illusions in this Ocean. We encounter many obstacles along the way. The Ocean is our thought, our common dream.

Salmon leave the ocean and come upstream because they want to go home. The wise salmon understands this. The wise salmon feels the energy that will bring her home. The salmon who is busy worrying "I can't jump that rock," or "Am I in the right stream?" is going to end up on somebody's dinner plate, says Juanita. Eyes closed, she sings to the heavens.

"As long as the grass is green, the salmon will swim upstream."

We listeners form a chorus. Our voices rise in the night.

"As long as the rivers shall flow," we harmonize, "as long as the grass is green, the salmon will swim upstream."

When it is over, Eve looks at me with a tired smile. Both of us are remembering the time at Diane's when Diane, Eve and I had all decided which animals reminded us of each other.

Sleek, exotic and troublesome, Diane would be perfect as an ocelot, we had laughed. I would be a deer, Eve insisted, because of my soulful eyes and my love of woodland places. And Eve would be a red salmon, Diane had proclaimed.

What? I had objected. Eve, a prehistoric old fish?

But Diane's cryptic reply had cut me short.

Eve is timeless, she had said. Eve is as old as the river.

When Eve reaches for my hand just now, in the fading evening light, I am filled with emotion.

☾ ☾ ☾

The clouds have blown over and the sky is bright with stars. Still energized from the powwow, Eve rests in my arms, using the walking stick to point out constellations of her own making. Oreos. Sneakers. Big Mama Salmon.

From across the campfire, Maggie and Karen's laughter fills the night. Their faces glow like burnished copper. It is midnight. I have brought the van to a secluded spot deep in the forest near Black Hawk, where the two have camped in their Bronco for the past week. Spring Festival has been a success for Maggie. She has made several thousand dollars from her pottery, with orders for more.

The mountain air is chilly as a breeze whips through the pines, sending sparks whirling high into the night. Bundled in blankets against the cold, we share Bluebird wine from old tin cups.

☾ ☾ ☾

We leave Valley of the Clouds late the next morning. Unable to wake up fully, Eve rides along beside me, mumbling cheerfully, nodding in and out of sleep. She is fine, she says, just very, very sleepy. I'm not surprised.

All day, we wind through the mountains, headed for the mysterious town of Vanishing Bridge, the place where I found the Loving Tree. Unfortunately, Vanishing Bridge does not appear on any map. And I never actually found the town, I remind Eve. As I recall, I became lost in the fog and stopped along the road to get my bearings, and that's when I noticed the Tree. Or Bennington noticed it, to be more accurate. But that whole morning was kind of a blur, and I'm not even sure where we're going now. It's beginning to look like we might be lost again.

It's late afternoon and we've stopped for a picnic. In our sweaters and mittens we spread a blanket beside a chattering stream and roast hot dogs over a fire. I study the map, looking for towns that might jog my memory. Cascade. Dexter. Buffalo Park. None of them sound quite right.

"We'll find it," says Eve.

We finish our lunch and head on. The map in her lap, Eve drifts in and out of dreams, talking in her sleep.

We drive for several hours. The shadows begin to stretch across the mountains. "We're lost," I say.

Eve's eyelids flutter. "Turn right up here," she says in a monotone.

"Huh? What for?"

"Didn't you tell me there was an Exxon somewhere near the Tree?"

"Well, sort of."

"Then turn. A sign back there said it was up ahead on the right a few miles."

"This is hopeless," I say, turning onto a narrow paved road.

Twenty minutes pass in silence, then Eve begins to snore. The road is bumpy and deserted, winding deeper and deeper into the forest.

"Now go left," says Eve, her eyes still closed.

"Whaaaat?" I ask, exasperated.

"I saw it. The sign for Vanishing Bridge. Go left."

"Eve, you're talking in your sleep," I mutter. But strangely, there is a fork in the road just around the bend, and so I turn. What the hell.

Another twenty minutes pass. Bennington rests with her chin in Eve's lap.

"Slow down," says Eve, as we approach a clearing.

"I suppose you've seen another sign," I say doubtfully.

"Of course," she says. "Didn't you?"

I look over at her in surprise.

On our right, overlooking the river valley, is a grassy meadow. I slow down, and Bennington begins barking crazily, wanting out. Before I've managed to park, she scrambles out the window and races across the clearing.

"Good God," sputters Eve, her eyes opening wide. "What's happening?"

"I'm not sure," I say, patting her hand. "But I think we've found the Loving Tree."

☾ ☾ ☾

The meadow is perfectly still, and the click of the van doors sounds like cannons as we step down and stretch. Eve struggles with the sleeves of her wool Pendleton. A hawk circles lazily overhead as we cross the grassy clearing to where Bennington is sniffing vigorously around the base of the Tree.

We move slowly beneath a deep, clear sky.

"From here, it looks like nothing," Eve observes. "Like an old burned-up stump or something, just like you said."

We have come about halfway across the meadow. Pausing to catch her breath, Eve bends to admire wildflowers at our feet. Resting her weight on the walking stick, she picks one of the tiny blue and white flowers and holds it beneath my nose.

The centers of the petals are exactly the color of her eyes. As I inhale, the faint scent of early violets fills my head.

I reach for Eve and hold her to me. Her bones are as light as a kitten's, her face is pale as starlight.

"Put your arms around my neck," I say.

I lift Eve and carry her the remaining distance to the Loving Tree.

As we draw near, Eve extends her hand and caresses the bark. When she can see the figures within, her eyes widen.

"Oh, my God," she whispers.

"Do you think you can stand?"

"Yes," she says. Her breath is quick.

"Hold on to me. Hold on to your stick," I say, easing her onto the soft, mossy ground.

"I'm fine," she says distractedly. "My God," she repeats, "would you just look at that."

She moves close and embraces the tree. "Oh, this is exactly as I envisioned it."

Exquisitely formed within the gnarled stump of a burned-out tree trunk, two female figures, their legs and arms entwined, gaze skyward. They appear to be just moments from taking flight.

Carefully, Eve places her hand just above where their hearts would be. Her look is intent.

"Feel anything?" I ask.

"Yes. It's very warm," she says, and takes my hand and places it there. Despite the chill of late afternoon, the statue seems to glow with an inner life, and the feel of their faces, satiny smooth, is soft as a baby's skin.

Eve's face lights up and she grins at me. "The taller one winked at you just now, Sunny—did you see it?"

"She what?"

"Yes. I think she likes you."

Bennington rests on her haunches, smiling up at us, basking in the aura of peace and tranquility that emanates from this spot. Like a drug, it beguiles us.

Eve reaches for me, and her eyes burn like sapphires. Her kiss is tender and slow, like the coming of spring, but unmistakably wild. She slides a hand beneath my clothing, her hips caressing mine. Fingers and legs entwined, we breathe deeply of the moment, and of each other.

With only the sound of the wind through the trees, our spirits merge.

☾ ☾ ☾

Our supper consists of fruit, cheese, nuts, and Milky Way bars. Eve grumbles about the perils of being without a microwave. As we're eating, a family of deer considers us politely from their spot on the edge of the clearing, their coats thin and ragged, hard hit by winter.

Later, after dark, I pop us some popcorn over the campfire, and we huddle close, watching falling stars and listening to night sounds. Above our heads, the slender branch of a western hemlock whooshes in the wind. With just a hint of a smile on her lips, Eve asks which do I think is actually moving—is it the branch, or is it the wind?

There is a lengthy pause. Well, I muse, theoretically it could be either. It could be one just as well as the other. For example—

"Rrrrrrnt!" Eve buzzes, waving her hands. "Sorry Ma'am, your time's up. The correct answer, of course, is your mind! It's only your mind moving! Ha ha!"

"I should've known," I groan, as Eve howls with laughter.

When the moon is high and we can stay awake no longer, we cast a final glance in the direction of the Loving Tree and crawl off to bed.

"Think they'll come to life and fly tonight?" Eve asks, burrowing into piles of soft blankets in the back of the van.

"I don't know. Maybe you should keep watch," I joke.

"I'll try," she yawns. But as soon as her head touches the pillow, she's asleep, and I reach up on the wall above us and take down the dreamcatcher. I fan it once, twice, three times over Eve as blue moonlight settles across her features.

"I love you," I whisper, and somewhere from a far-off place, she mumbles—

"I love you more."

Holding her tightly, I can feel the tears as they slide down my cheek and onto the pillow, one by one like notes in music.

☾ ☾ ☾

It is twilight, the air is cool. I stand watching the end of a day as the sky across the mountaintops fades from deep rose to lavender.

On the other side of the meadow, a figure skirts my vision. It is an old woman. Her hair is white, her posture bent. Her back is toward me. She appears to be ripping branches from a tree.

Curious, I draw near. I can see the veins in her hands protruding with every pull. Slowly I discern the rough, scaly bark of the tree, the gnarled roots, that special stance. Why, the woman is ravaging the Loving Tree!

"Hey," I demand angrily. "What do you think you're doing?"

Calmly, almost as if she had been expecting me, the old woman turns. She is flushed and out of breath. Brushing a long strand of hair from her eyes, she smiles a sad little smile.

"You must think me very foolish," she says. "I've been coming to this tree every spring for over fifty years. I love to watch the sunsets. But now," she sighs, and her hands tremble, "now, I'm just not as young as I used to be."

I can see that she has not been tugging at branches after all, but at vines, vines that are strangling the Loving Tree. They lay in tangled heaps at our feet. I stare at them uncomfortably for what seems an eternity.

"No," I say to the old woman quietly. "I don't think you're foolish at all."

And then, rolling up my sleeves, I step closer.

"Let me help you," I say.

A feeling of indescribable love washes over me as her eyes meet mine.

☾ ☾ ☾

My waking comes gently, like a breeze passing through a gossamer curtain. Beside me, Eve's eyelids flutter and she smiles. Bennington snores happily at our feet. Pearly dawn light fills the van.

"Were you dreaming?" I whisper.

"Yes," replies Eve, pressing herself warmly against me. She smiles happily, and in a slow, deep, theatrical voice, says, "My dear, they're as alive as you allow them to be." She giggles. She stretches and yawns.

"Who?" I ask. "Who's alive?"

"Oh, those two in the tree. Their skin was so soft and their faces so warm that I said, 'Why, they're alive!' An old woman was standing there, and she turned to me and said, 'They're as alive as you allow them to be.'"

☾ ☾ ☾

While deer nibble popcorn by the edge of the meadow, Eve feeds chipmunks by the Loving Tree.

I imagine extravagant birds lighting in her hair, wild beasts resting their chins in her lap, mountain lions purring tenderly at her feet.

I don't want this day to end.

☾ ☾ ☾

We have driven all night; the thwack of windshield wipers and the hum of wet tires are hypnotic. Eve is scheduled to see her physician at ten in the morning. We should make it back to Renfield just in time.

Wrapped in a blanket, the remains of a half-eaten banana in her hand, Eve snores lightly. She jerks awake when it thunders, and gives me a puzzled look.

"Sunny," she whispers, "was it a dream?"

"No," I reply, reaching for her hand. "It was not a dream."

She smiles weakly and drifts back to sleep.

18

Before I attacked it with the hedge trimmers last summer, it was wild and overgrown and I hadn't recognized it for what it was. Now, on Easter Sunday, the forsythia blooms brightly, shines like a wall of buttered corn.

I'm planting flowers this afternoon. Eve sits on the porch swing watching as I pack dirt around the roots and the tender leaves of a bronze petunia.

She wears faded Levis and a baggy white sweatshirt and her hair is in pigtails. A wool plaid blanket is draped like a shawl across her shoulders. There's a smudge of dirt on her chin. She listens to birds, rests.

No hurry.

I learn to hang on to these moments.

☾ ☾ ☾

Today Eve felt well enough to keep me company as I worked on revisions. She lay on the sofa, sometimes dreaming, sometimes waking, sometimes editing my work as I read it out loud, hearing things I can't or won't, shaming me with her precision and timing, her flair for rhythm and grace.

Her eyes glisten and her hand trembles as she reaches up, runs a finger over my fly. One of the buttons has come undone. She winks.

Love those 501s, says her smile. Used to rip them open, yank them off of you with one hand.

With great effort she pulls me close and holds me, the pulse beating at her brow.

☾ ☾ ☾

This morning Eve is sitting up in bed, surrounded by pillows.

"Who is Walt Disney!" she shouts. Then, "What is New Zealand," followed by "What is a xylophone!"

"Hey," she grins, as I enter the room. Her face is flushed, her eyes glassy. "Want to play Jeopardy?"

She stares at the TV, which is not on.

"Not right now," I say, feeling her forehead.

"Sunny," she says brightly, "I had some visitors last night."

"Oh?" I ask, taking her pulse. It is racing.

"We tried to be quiet but oh, there was so much to talk about. They said not to worry, it's going to be all right."

"Of course it is," I say.

"Like dreaming. They said it's going to be just like dreaming, only different."

"Eve, you have a fever. Will you drink some of this special tea Mary brewed for you? Will you do that for me?" I unscrew the lid and slip a straw inside.

She drinks.

"Good. Now some more," I coax. The tea is lavender and smells wonderfully herbal.

She manages a swallow or two, then falls back on her pillow, exhausted, distracted.

"They wanted me to go with them." she rambles.

"Who?" I ask. "Who wanted you to go with them?"

"...but I said I wanted to say goodbye to you first, and

to Olga, and Diane, and they said no, I couldn't, it doesn't work that way."

"Eve, what are you saying?" I ask, wishing Betty, the nurse, were here.

"I'm surprised you didn't hear us, Sunny. We were up all night. It was a party. Mom and Gerry and David. Even Grandma Phillips was here."

Sweaty and bloodshot, I stare at her blankly, unable to cope.

"That's nice, honey," I mumble.

When Betty arrives at noon, Eve is asleep. Her temperature is normal, her breathing has quieted.

☾ ☾ ☾

I'm not going to let them take her.

At bedtime I shower and join Eve in her bed.

I'm not going to let them take her, I vow.

"I'll read," I say, "till you fall asleep. I'm going to stay right here with you tonight."

"I can't promise I'll do anything," she grins.

I read aloud from Jeanette Winterson's *The Passion.*

As Eve is drifting off I tell her to be sure and wake me if her brother or her mother come visit during the night.

She opens her eyes and a troubled look clouds her fine features.

"How can they?" she asks quite simply, looking puzzled. "They're dead."

☾ ☾ ☾

What began as a sniffle in the middle of the night progresses to a cough by morning, a rattle by noon.

When Fran, Della and I drive her to the hospital, Eve is

diagnosed with pneumonia.

Diane, Marcy and I go to an AIDS support group. We meet some kind and compassionate people. I drink coffee till my mouth tastes like mud. It's good to be someplace where it's okay to be needy, okay to be scared.

Eve has refused AZT, calls it poison. She never speaks of those days in Mexico with her father. Diane thinks Bradley went there in search of a miracle cure, and found none.

After several days Eve's condition has improved, and she gets to come home. Fran and I string up a welcome home banner for her.

☾ ☾ ☾

The nosebleeds began about a week ago, while she was walking in her sleep. But the sleepwalking has been a fairly regular thing since right after she started getting the shakes so bad, which came shortly after her release from the hospital the first time, I think.

Bradley was here last week. He stayed at Eve's, which is where I'm staying, though of course most of my stuff is still at the apartment.

The first nosebleed was pretty bad. It was pretty messy. We're not sure if she banged into something or what. I heard a noise in the night in the kitchen and had gone out to check, and found Eve standing up on a chair in the dark trying to comb her hair with a fork.

I led her back to bed and it wasn't till she had lain down that I noticed the blood all down the front of her gown, smeared on her hands. It was everywhere, the sheets, the pillowcase. I don't think Eve fully woke up throughout the entire incident.

Bradley looked tired. He brought us a pound of Jamaica Blue Mountain coffee. Eve thinks it's wimpy, says it tastes like tea, but I kind of like it. She was trying to talk to me about mutual funds, shares in AT&T. I said no, please, not just now, and went to Diane's, and stood in her living room looking at all her books. It makes me feel good to look at all Diane's books.

Diane came in, was trying to talk to me about a house, a car, some property. No, I said. Yes, she said, and took me by the arm, but there was dried blood all over my sleeve, and both of us just stood there, staring at it.

Before Bradley flew back to San Francisco he made tentative arrangements at Hospice Care. Eve doesn't need to go to a hospice, I said. I'm here.

"Just think about it, Sunny," he said. "I'll be back in a few weeks."

And when we hugged he was shaking like a leaf.

This afternoon, Holly Kaufman was over.

Beneficiary, she said.

Not now, I said.

☾ ☾ ☾

She sits at the kitchen table in her blue silk robe drinking tea through a straw from the handsome mug that was our gift from Maggie. It makes a solid, clinking sound when she sets it on her saucer.

Out in the dining room, Diane is fiddling with the CD player and puts on something I've not heard before. It fills the house with autumn noises, whirling leaves, wind whistling down alleys in the dead of night.

She comes into the kitchen, sits down with us at the table. She looks haggard. Deep creases line her eyes and her mouth.

"How ya doin', Pussy?" she asks, squeezing Eve's hand.

Eve looks up slowly, smiles in recognition.

"You bending spoons with your mind again?" Diane jokes, stooping to pick up some mangled silverware off the floor. I have no idea how long it's been there.

"Kid stuff," Eve says with fiercely concentrated effort, playing along. "See what I can do when I really try."

She motions with her eyes out the window to the barbecue grill she ran over last summer, and the three of us laugh until tears well up in our eyes.

☾ ☾ ☾

Death brings with it a mood, fragile and tender.

I remember holding Diane's hand at the funeral as someone spoke of the bricks of experience, and how we use them to build our lives.

Or rebuild them, as the case may be.

I thought back to a starry night in summer on the porch with a bottle of wine.

"Did you know," Eve had asked joyfully, lightheartedly, "Did you know that from the bottom of a well you can see the stars shining even during the day?"

Is that true, I wondered? And if so, how very like you to shine through the darkness of your passing with an image of light. Does Cassiopeia, your favorite, still burn brightly for you now? Or the Milky Way—path of souls? Like a footprint or an echo, the dissolving trace of a memory passing by.

After the funeral I went home to live with my family. Eventually I went back to school, taught for a while, ran the family bookstore, took some time off to travel. With my inheritance from Eve, I was pretty much free to do as I pleased. It was a nice arrangement for an unambitious writer.

Diane and I remained close. Her agent became my agent, and through the years I've gotten some nice reviews on the work that Eve and I did at the end.

Recently, Diane and Mother spent some time in Indonesia. They're collaborating on a new book called *Samsara*. The word originates from Sanskrit and refers to the indefinitely repeated cycles of birth, misery and death caused by karma.

I think about this sometimes, and wonder what roads, what forms all of us will take in our future lives, and if perhaps we might be spared some of the anguish, some of the loss next time.

The dreamcatcher still hangs above my bed. For brief moments, in the lonely hours of the spirit, it enables me to enter sacred time. In the land of dreams, I am with her. Like a mountain or like the sun, she's always there. It is I who fade in and out of the valley. And it's beautiful, walking in the sun down that long yellow wall of summer.

Love conquers all, Eve. Until next time.

The End

MORE FICTION TO STIR THE IMAGINATION
FROM
RISING TIDE PRESS

RETURN TO ISIS
Jean Stewart
It is the year 2093, and Whit, a bold woman warrior from an Amazon nation, rescues Amelia from a dismal world where females are either breeders or drones. During their arduous journey back to the shining all-women's world of Artemis, they are unexpectedly drawn to each other. This engaging first book in the trilogy has it all—romance, mystery, and adventure.
Nominated for a 1993 Lambda Literary Award
ISBN 0-9628938-6-2; 192 Pages; $9.99

ISIS RISING
Jean Stewart
In this stirring romantic fantasy, the familiar cast of lovable characters begin to rebuild the colony of Isis, burned to the ground ten years earlier by the dread Regulators. But evil forces threaten to destroy their dream. A swashbuckling futuristic adventure and an endearing love story all rolled into one. ISBN 0-9628938-8-9; 192 Pages; $9.95

WARRIORS OF ISIS
Jean Stewart
At last, the third lusty tale of high adventure and passionate romance among the Freeland Warriors. Arinna Sojourner, the evil product of genetic engineering, vows to destroy the fledgling colony of Isis with her incredible psychic powers. Whit, Kali, and other warriors battle to save their world, in this novel bursting with life, love, heroines and villains.
Nominated for a 1995 Lambda Literary Award
ISBN 1-883061-03-2; 256 Pages; $10.99

DEADLY RENDEZVOUS: A Toni Underwood Mystery
Diane Davidson
A string of brutal murders in the middle of the desert plunges Lieutenant Toni Underwood and her lover Megan into a high profile investigation which uncovers a world of drugs, corruption and murder, as well as the dark side of the human mind. An explosive, fast-paced, action-packed whodunit.
ISBN 1-883061-02-4; 224 pages; $9.99

LOVESPELL
Karen Williams
A deliciously erotic and humorous love story in which Kate Gallagher, a shy veterinarian, and Allegra, who has magic at her fingertips, fall in love. A masterful blend of fantasy and reality, this beautifully written story will warm your heart and delight your imagination.
ISBN 0-9628938-2-X; 192 Pages; $9.95

DANGER IN HIGH PLACES: An Alix Nicholson Mystery
Sharon Gilligan
Set against the backdrop of Washington, DC., this riveting mystery introduces freelance photographer and amateur sleuth, Alix Nicholson. Alix stumbles on a deadly scheme surrounding AIDS funding, and with the help of a lesbian Congressional aide, unravels the mystery.
ISBN 0-9628938-7-0; 176 Pages, $9.95

DANGER! CROSS CURRENTS: AN Alix Nicholson Mystery
Sharon Gilligan
The exciting sequel to *Danger in High Places* brings freelance photographer Alix Nicholson face-to-face with an old love and a murder. When Alix's landlady, a real estate developer, turns up dead, and her much younger lover, Leah Claire, is the prime suspect, Alix launches a frantic campaign to find the real killer. ISBN 1-883061-01-6; 192 Pages; $9.99

YOU LIGHT THE FIRE
Kristen Garrett
Here's a grown-up **Rubyfruit Jungle**—sexy, spicy, and sidesplittingly funny. Take a gorgeous, sexy, high school math teacher and put her together with a raunchy, commitment-shy, ex-rock singer, and you've got a hilarious, unforgettable love story. ISBN 0-9628938-5-4; $9.95

NO WITNESSES
Nancy Sanra
This cliff-hanger of a mystery set in San Francisco, introduces Detective Tally McGinnis, the brains and brawn behind the Phoenix Detective Agency. But Tally is no great sleuth at protecting her own heart. And so, when her ex-lover Pamela Tresdale is arrested for the grisly murder of a wealthy Texas heiress, Tally rushes to the rescue. Despite friends' warnings, Tally is drawn once again into Pamela's web of deception and betrayal, as she attempts to clear her and find the real killer. A gripping whodunit. ISBN 1-883061-05-9; 192 Pages; $9.99

CORNERS OF THE HEART
Leslie Grey
A captivating novel of love and suspense in which beautiful French-born Chris Benet and Katya Michaels meet and fall in love. But their budding love is shadowed by a vicious killer, whom they must outwit. Your heart will pound as the story races to its heart-stopping conclusion.
ISBN 0-9628938-3-8; 224 pages; $9.95

SHADOWS AFTER DARK
Ouida Crozier
Wings of death spread over the world of Kornagy, and Kyril's mission on Earth is to find the cure. Here she meets and falls in love with Kathryn, who is horrified to learn that her mysterious, darkly exotic lover is a vampire. This tender love story is the ultimate lesbian vampire novel!
ISBN 1-883061-50-4; 224 Pages; $9.95

HEARTSTONE AND SABER
Jacqui Singleton
You can almost hear the sabers clash in this rousing tale of good and evil, of passionate love, of warrior queens and white witches. Cydell, the imperious queen of Mauldar, and Elayna, the Fair Witch of Avoreed join forces to combat the evil that menaces the empire, and in the course of doing that, find rapturous love.
ISBN 1-883061-00-8; 224 Pages; $10.99

EDGE OF PASSION
Shelley Smith
This sizzling novel about an all-consuming love affair between a younger and an older woman is set in colorful Provincetown. A gripping love story, which is both fierce and tender, it will keep you breathless until the last page. ISBN 0-9628938-1-1; 192 Pages; $8.95

How To Order:
Rising Tide Press books are available from you local women's bookstore or directly from Rising Tide Press. Send check, money order, or Visa/MC account number, with expiration date and signature to: Rising Tide Press, 5 Kivy St., Huntington Sta., New York 11746. Credit card orders must be over $25. Remember to include shipping and handling charges: $4.95 for 1-3 books, plus $1.00 for each additional book. Credit Card Orders Call our Toll Free # 1-800-648-5333. For UPS delivery, provide street address.